THE HAWAIIAN ISLAND DETECTIVE CLUB SERIES

Menehunes Missing

BY Cheryl Linn Martin

Comfort PUBLISHING

For information, address Comfort Publishing, 296 Church St. N., Concord, NC 28025. The views expressed in this book are not necessarily those of the publisher.

First printing

Book cover design
by Reed Karriker

ISBN: 978-1-938388-24-8
Published by Comfort Publishing, LLC
www.comfortpublishing.com

Printed in the United States of America

To my sister-in-law, Evelyn,
for her inspiration.

had purchased books were carrying them into library. I had one student tell me she has already read it all the way through one time and is in the process of reading it a second time because "it is soooo good!" — C. Reed, Librarian

"I love this book — my favorite book! The best thing about it is the mystery." — Annika

"I am totally a fan of you!" — Amanda

"Your book is awesome!" — Jadon

"We love your book so far!" — Nakkita
(the class is reading it at school)

"This is a very good book with some excellent morals we can learn from: like treating your siblings with love and respecting your parents. I really liked Leilani and felt her loss and victories." — Maddie

Reviewers:

"When I was a middle school teacher, my students would have loved this book. Do you want to get your children, grandchildren, or neighborhood youngsters hooked on reading good books this school year? Then you'll want to grab this great middle-grade mystery." — Davalynn Spencer

"This is such a fun story! An adventure-mystery set in Hawaii where the kids have to solve the crime—what's NOT to love?! It's the kind of adventure I drooled about having when I was in middle school. Even as an adult, I couldn't wait for the next chapter!" — *Emily C. Reynolds*

"Fun, exciting, and well-written. The characters are well-developed, and the plot is exciting. I read the book in two days (while homeschooling and writing!) – I enjoyed it that much." — *Danika Cooley*

"Cheryl has a way with writing for Middle Readers, but little does she know, she has this writer hooked on the mysteries as well." — *Linda Glaz*

"The description and lure of the Hawaiian setting is so great it gives readers a chance to feel like they're walking on the beaches in their flip-flops." — *Sophie Cuffe*

"A Nancy Drew-style story for the twenty-first century — packed with investigative fun that will bring young readers back for more adventures with *The Hawaiian Island Detective Club.*" — *Jill Williamson*

Acknowledgements

Above all, I give my gratitude and praise to God who has been with me every step, no matter how difficult, along this amazing writing journey.

Thank you, everyone who purchased, gifted, and read *Pineapples in Peril*. Your support means everything to me!

I again extend my thanks to my husband, Harrison, my children, Ian, Ashley and Shane, and my son-in-law, Dave, for all their support as I continue to write, edit and market—while many times ignoring housework and cooking!

Thank you, Hartline Literary agents, Terry Burns, who represents me, and Linda Glaz who critiques and supports my writing.

Success for any author lies not only in an interesting, well-written story, but in marketing support. I owe so much to those who endorsed, posted, tweeted, blogged and reviewed book one, Pineapples in Peril — Karla Akins, Max Elliot Anderson, Gail Bauginet, Danika Cooley, Sadie and Sophie Cuffe, Lena Nelson Dooley, Camille Eide, Miralee Ferrell, Lynne Gentry, Kellie Gilbert, Linda Glaz, Emily Hendrickson, Casey Herringshaw, Lisa Lickel, Jessica Nelson, Patricia Rushford, Lynda Schab, Davalynn Spencer, Sharon Srock, Barbara Warren and Jill Williamson. Thank you, Columbian and Camas/Washougal Post Record for your amazing, supportive articles, and thank you, Jason Huddle, for discovering every review and article about *Pineapples in Peril* and posting the links and wonderful comments on Facebook.

I spent time during the summer visiting several Portland Parks and Recreation community centers as a guest instructor for day camps. Thank you, Southwest, East Portland, Hillside, Fulton, and Montavilla Community Centers, staff, camp leaders and kids for your gracious support and excitement about my books.

School librarians, counselors and teachers have been so supportive of my writing and not only have I spoken at several, I also have more scheduled after the release of *Menehunes Missing*. Thank you, King's Way, Cornerstone, Gause and Riverview. A special thanks to Kalama Intermediate and Kamalii Elementary for inviting me to visit while I was in Hawaii.

Thank you, members of American Christian Fiction Writers, Oregon Christian Writers, and the Portland Chapter of ACFW, for all your support, instruction, and opportunities.

Cover art is vital to the success of any book — especially when you're trying to attract kids. Thank you, Reed Karriker, for your amazing book covers.

And, finally, thank you, Kristy Huddle, and everyone at Comfort Publishing who were willing to take the risk with a new author, and publish *The Hawaiian Island Detective Club* series.

Pronunciation Help for Some of the Hawaiian Words Used in Menehunes Missing

Character Names

Leilani is pronounced: lay-LAH-nee
Kimo is pronounced: KEE-moh
Akamai is pronounced: ah-kah-MY
Maile is pronounced: MY-lee
Kainoa is pronounced: ky-NO-ah (ky rhymes with sky.)
Luana is pronounced: lu-AHN-ah
Onakea is pronounced: oh-nah-KAY-ah
Yamada is pronounced: yah-MAH-dah

Other Words
(and Some Meanings)

Akaka Falls is pronounced: ah-KAH-kah
Meaning: A beautiful, high waterfall on the Big Island (Hawaii.)

Lanai is pronounced: la-NY (NY rhymes with sky.)
Meaning: A porch or veranda.

Luau is pronounced: LOO-au (au rhymes with cow.)
Meaning: A Hawaiian feast.

Menehune is pronounced: meh-neh-HOO-neh
Meaning: The mythical Hawaiian little people (similar to Leprechauns) who built roads, ponds and other structures at night. Even though the Menehune are considered mythical, it is believed among many people that the stories were based around a group of island inhabitants who were quite small and very hard workers.

Pau Hana is pronounced: pow-HAH-nah
Meaning: Work is done for the day.

Pipeline is a famous surfing beach on the North Shore of the island of Oahu.

Saimin Noodles is pronounced: SY-min (SY rhymes with sky)
Meaning: A popular noodle soup in Hawaii.

Slippers is used in Hawaii the same as flip-flops.

Spouting Horn on Kauai is pronounced: cow-EYE or cow-AH-ee (most mainlanders tend to use the first)
Meaning: A place on the island of Kauai where the water spurts high in the air through the rocks when waves hit.

Ekahi
(One)

I smoothed the crumpled paper, stared at the words, and read the first clue.

I'm Menehune Number One. Find and check me out if you can.
I'm hiding amongst kids and cords.

Maile Onakea and Sam Bennett, my best friends, suddenly burst into my room.

Sam jumped onto my bed, his shaggy blonde hair flopping around like palm fronds in the wind. "Did you get it? I'm crazy pumped about this whole Menehune Hunt thing. Bet no matter how hard the clue is, you've already figured it out, huh? Come on, Leilani! Read that puppy out loud."

Maile giggled. "Sam, you're insane." She also plopped onto my bed, tucked a strand of her long hair behind an ear, and locked dark brown eyes on mine. "So, what does it say?"

I ignored her question. "You guys sure got here fast."

"My mom and I picked up Sam, then came straight over. Mom thinks it's cool we're doing the statue search thing."

I nodded. "So does mine. She says the money raised will really help the school. Guess there's been a couple hundred people who've already paid the entry fee."

I pictured myself starting eighth grade with a computer room full of brand new equipment.

Sam groaned. "Okay, so everyone's mom is happy. No need to party about it. Show us the clue. Let's get on this wave and ride it all the way. We have a totally great chance of winning because we're amazing at solving stuff. Just like the whole pineapple mystery. So, get on it, Leilani. We're waiting."

"I will if you'll stop babbling for a minute."

"Whatever."

I loved Sam's endless talking. It entertained me, but it also motivated me. Today was no different. I really wanted to do the Menehune Hunt and to be the first to find all eight of the little statues. It wasn't a real mystery, but I'd use the same skills to figure out the clues.

"Okay. Here it is." I read aloud to my friends.

I'm Menehune Number One. Find and check me out if you can.
I'm hiding amongst kids and cords.

Sam stared at me, his face scrunched as if he'd just sucked on a lemon.

Maile grimaced. "What a crazy clue. We'll never figure it out."

I shrugged. "I think that's the point. It's not supposed to be totally easy to find these Menehune statues." I dug in my pocket for the other piece of paper. "They gave me this when I signed up today. It's the rules." I smoothed the page and read aloud. "Eight of Hawaii's treasured *little people* are hiding in our town. Because no one has ever captured a Menehune, we will be using statues of them. Help us find all eight using the clues provided. No one can begin searching until three o'clock on Day One."

Maile craned her neck to see the paper. "But we can guess where to look, right?"

"Yeah. But it says anyone who gets to the location before three o'clock today will be given a penalty."

Sam's head tipped to one side. "A penalty?"

"Yup. Twenty-four hours. They won't get the next clue until the following day at three o'clock." I fingered the paper and stared at the words. "So let's see if we can figure out the first clue."

My two friends scooted close.

"Hmm. Kids and cords." I sighed. "Has to be someplace where there's lots of tech stuff."

Maile nodded. "All I can think of is a computer store."

"Not many kids there."

"Yeah, guess not."

The bed jiggled when Sam shifted his position. "Maybe someplace where lots of kids hang out. Like the beach or a park —"

"Or school, or a video game store." Maile sat upright, her eyes lighting up like little candles. "That's it! A video game store. There are lots of cords to run all the screens and gaming stuff. You know, like the boxes and the controllers."

"Super idea." I smiled. It would be great if we could get to the first statue before anyone else. I'd spent my summer unable to surf because of a broken arm. Solving the mystery at the Tong Pineapple Plantation with my two friends had kept me not only busy, but sane. Tomorrow my cast was coming off, so I could finally get some surfing in before school started. And finding all the menehune statues would be a great ending to the summer.

Sam's lips curved and he slapped a hand on his thigh. "Then Island Games it is."

"Yeah." I nodded. "But let's think of some other possibilities too. Just in case it's not there."

Maile shrugged. "Sounds good to me."

"So, where else would there be a lot of kids and cords?" I leaned back into pillows, gazed at my feet, and tried to think of another place.

Sam rubbed his forehead as if deep in thought. "No cords at the beach or in the park. What about school?" He jerked upright, his voice raising to a higher pitch. "Maybe the computer room. There are about a b'zillion outlets all over, and tons of cords."

I sighed. "Yeah, you're right, and that's a great idea, but since school hasn't started yet, only the office is open. No kids."

"Oh yeah." Sam slunk down onto the bed.

"Don't give up." Maile nudged him. "Keep thinking of ideas. We're not going to find the first Menehune until we come up with a solution to the clue and the correct location."

"Hmm. It still could be at the school." I leaned forward. "What if the clue doesn't mean that there have to be kids there right now, but just a place which can be filled with kids and cords? Maybe the statue is sitting right outside the door, or maybe they've unlocked all the rooms and it's hidden someplace inside with the computers."

Maile sat up and grinned. "Good idea, Leilani. So, we all agree, right? We'll check out Island Games first, and if we don't find the Menehune, we'll go on to the school, okay?"

Sam nodded. "You got it."

I high-fived my two friends. "Let's get our bikes and go into town. I'm sure my mom will give you guys a ride home and then we can meet on the main road by the church about two-thirty. Sound good?"

Maile nodded and grabbed my right hand.

Sam hesitated, rolled his eyes, and finally grabbed my fingers. "Can't wait 'til you get this stupid cast off."

Maile's face lit up as she yelped. "Let's go, Hawaiian Island Detective Club!"

I shot her a sideways glance and shook my head.

She shrugged and returned an I-don't-care glare. "We're still the club, except we solve real crimes now."

Sam nodded. "I guess it's okay we still call it a club. This Menehune Hunt will totally give us practice until another way cool real mystery pops up."

"Yeah. You never know when intrigue might come our way." I grinned. "Let's go talk to my mom about your rides home."

Excitement oozed from my friends. They probably felt it from me too.

We jumped off the bed and maneuvered to my bedroom door. But before I grabbed the knob …

Screeeeech! … Thud!

Elua
(Two)

My heart tried to escape its ribbed prison. I gulped.

Sam jumped. "What was that?" His eyes grew big and round like two full moons.

I clutched the knob, jerked open the bedroom door, and spotted the drop-down ladder from the attic. Kimo climbed toward the black hole above. "Hey, dork-boy, you let the ladder bang down and hit the floor."

"Man, that thing is creepy noisy." Maile stepped forward and inspected the contraption.

Planting both hands onto my hips, I watched as my little brother snaked up the rungs. "What are you doing?"

"Looking for an inner tube for my bike. Mine popped."

"You think there's one in the attic?"

He disappeared into the dark void. "Uh huh." The light turned on. "Dad didn't like all the junk we had under the back lanai, so he moved it up here."

A smile spread across my lips. Dad was such a neat-nick. I'd missed him every day since he'd died.

"Found it!" The light in the attic dimmed and Kimo's legs appeared out of the black as he stepped backward down the ladder. "Now I can fix my tire."

"You going bike riding with your friends?"

"Nope."

I wrinkled my nose. What was Kimo up to?

He stepped off the last rung. "I'm going with you guys to find the Menehune."

"Kimo! You were spying on us, you little rat."

"See? I'm a good detective."

I grimaced. "Yeah. I already told you that, but this is a fundraiser for our school, not yours. You're not coming with us."

"Mahhhhhhm! Leilani's being mean to me." His ten-year-old shriek hurt my ears.

Clamping an arm and a cast across my chest, I glared at my irritating little brother. Just because he helped me with the pineapple case didn't mean he could come with me and my friends all the time.

Mom appeared in the hallway and marched toward us. "What is it this time, Kimo?"

"Leilani and Maile and Sam are riding bikes into town to look for the first Menehune. They won't let me come."

She sighed. "Kimo, you're not going with them. Let your sister and her friends do this by themselves. It's for their school."

Kimo stomped his foot. "Not fair!" He could be such a baby sometimes.

I cocked my head and shot him an I'm-so-right smirk.

He stuck out his tongue and tramped down the hall past Mom, the inner-tube swinging at his side. I couldn't help but feel a twinge of guilt. He had helped us a lot with the pineapple mystery.

I sighed. *Dear Lord, what can I do to involve Kimo?* Maybe he could help figure out the clues, but not tag along with us. I hoped that would make him happy.

I focused on Mom. "Could you give Maile and Sam a ride home? They need to get their bikes so we can go to town."

"Sure." She passed me a sly glance. "Figure out the first clue already?"

"Maybe. We have a theory anyway."

"Well, good luck." Mom sauntered toward the living room. Then she stopped, turned, and faced me. "Whatever you do over the next couple days, you need to plan around your appointment tomorrow morning to get your cast off."

"I will." Seriously? I'd been dying to get the gross thing off. It almost ruined my entire summer. And the itching drove me crazy. I could hardly wait for tomorrow.

"Good." She motioned for Maile and Sam to follow her. "Let's get you two home."

"Thanks, Mrs. Akamai." Maile padded down the hall, Sam trudging behind.

I followed them out of the house and to the SUV.

"You coming along for the ride?" Mom hoisted herself into the big truck.

"Nah. I have some stuff to do." Yeah, like thinking about other possible answers to the clue and planning my surfing come-back once the horrible cast was gone.

Waving goodbye, I watched Mom back the truck.

Kimo appeared on the lanai. "You're going to miss my help, 'cause I know a lot of things and I'm a super good detective."

I frowned. "Yeah, yeah, you've told me that about a b'zillion times already."

"That's 'cause you won't believe it."

I shook my head, moved onto the lanai, and looked him in the eye. "I do believe it." I rubbed my temple. "Why don't you help us decipher the clues?"

He smiled. "Really?"

"But you can't tag along once we go searching, okay?"

He twisted his mouth to the side and squirmed a little. "Okay, I guess so."

"Good." I hugged him.

"You squeeze hard, Leilani." He laughed.

I released my grip and poked him in the chest. "Yup. Come on inside. Let's surprise Mom and fix lunch."

"Cool." Kimo galloped through the door and bee-lined it to the kitchen. He opened a cupboard and pulled out a box of macaroni and cheese. "Let's cook this."

"Sure. I'll make a salad." The bin in the fridge was full of lettuce and other veggies.

Kimo tore open the box. "When you leaving to find the first statue?"

"Not until three o'clock."

"My teacher tells us stories about the Menehune. She said they're Hawaiian little people, kinda like leprechauns. They worked at night building stuff like ponds and roads."

"Yup. She's right."

Kimo set the table while I boiled the macaroni and stirred in the butter, cheese and milk.

He skipped to the cupboard next to me and strained to reach the shelf. "When can I see the clue? I bet I'll figure out the answer."

"I'll show you after lunch." Watching his little fingers grope for a glass, I offered help. "Here. Let me get those." I put down the spoon and grabbed three glasses. "Why don't you pour the milk?" I set the pasta aside and reached for a bowl. A few pieces of torn lettuce and some tomato slices made a great salad.

"Oops!" Kimo's shout caught my attention.

I turned and spotted the milky mess on the table. Shaking my head, I grabbed a dishrag. "Here, Kimo. Wipe up your spill."

The front screen banged and Mom ambled into the kitchen. "Mmm." She sniffed the air. "Smells like macaroni and cheese."

Kimo beamed. "I picked it out and helped Leilani. She cooked and I set the table."

Mom ran her hand along the outside of one of the glasses and then stared at the white slime. "You pour the milk too?"

"Yup."

She chuckled and wiped the wet finger on a napkin.

As we settled at the table, visions of the time I tried to cook stir-fry, and burned the entire dinner paraded through my head. Macaroni and cheese was a lot easier.

After we devoured lunch and cleared the table, I loaded the dishwasher. Kimo scampered to his room.

Mom lowered her chin and narrowed her eyes. "How did you manage to make things okay with your brother? He was pretty mad this morning."

I tucked a plate into the wire rack and shrugged. "I told him he could help me figure out the clues. But he can't tag along with us."

Mom grinned. "Sounds fair to me." She slipped her hand under my chin, lifted, and locked her eyes on mine. "Thanks for making Kimo feel part of the things you do. He admires everything about you."

"Don't know why."

Mom pulled her hand from my chin and folded both arms across her chest. "Think about it, Leilani. He hates the water and you're the big surfer of the family. You also have more of your dad's Hawaiian characteristics." She allowed a slight grin to come across her face. "And he really misses him."

I nodded, then loaded the last dish. We all missed Dad. But at least I was older than Kimo when he'd died. Dad had always said that God gave us wonderful blessings. Dad himself had been one for us.

I placed the last glass in the top rack. "I'm going to get ready to meet Maile and Sam."

"Okay. Good luck with the search."

I trekked down the hall and into my room. Kimo was lying on his stomach across my bed, his legs bent, and his feet waving around. "Kimo! What are you doing in here? You know you're not allowed." I stomped to the far side and grabbed the paper he was gawking at.

"You said I could read the clue and help figure it out."

"Yeah, but I didn't say you could just come into my room anytime you wanted."

"But you're going to be so happy." He sat upright and beamed.

"Doubt that. I'm pretty mad." I pointed toward the door. "Get out of here right now before I tell Mom."

He shook his head, the grin still consuming his face. "Nope. I won't."

I blasted a fiery stare at my brother. "Yes —"

"I know the answer to the clue."

I gritted my teeth. Yes, Kimo looked up to me, but why did I have to take his annoying meddling in my life? "We've already figured it out."

"You did?" He frowned. "So what's your answer?"

I shouldn't tell him, but if I didn't, he'd bother me forever and think I really didn't know the solution. "It's at Island Games. And if it's not there, it's in the school computer room."

His frown morphed into a smirk. "Nope. You're wrong."

Ekolu
(Three)

I glared at Kimo. "Oh, yeah? So, what's your answer?"

"Not telling."

"Oh great. I give you a chance to help us and now you don't want to. What's up with that?"

Kimo stared at me, his lips pinched tight.

"Okay. Be that way." I grabbed my backpack and my cell, and marched toward the bathroom. "I'm leaving to meet Maile and Sam. You need to get OUT of my room."

Kimo tromped into the hallway, but not before he had the last word. "You'll see. You won't find the Menehune and then you'll have to come ask me where it is." He stuck out his tongue and continued the pounding footsteps toward his room.

Once I was sure Kimo was far away, I plodded to my bed and snatched the clue. I read it over and over. What did he see in the thing? I pressed my lips together, folded the paper, and stuck the clue in my pocket. Maile, Sam and I were right. The first Menehune was at Island Games or the school computer room.

I made my way to the bathroom and brushed my teeth. Excitement bubbled in my stomach. Tossing the wet brush and half empty tube into a drawer, I grinned. What a great end to my summer — a new mystery and my cast removed. 'Course we hadn't solved the Menehune Hunt yet. And it wasn't a real mystery, but I figured it counted.

Kimo sat on the couch, his face contorted and arms clamped across his chest. I plunked down next to him. "Sorry, kiddo."

He stared straight ahead.

I swallowed hard. "I'm leaving now."

He didn't move.

"Tell you what, why don't I call when we find the first Menehune?"

Kimo squirmed and riveted his eyes on mine. "You won't find it."

I sighed. "Okay." What should I say? He totally believed that we wouldn't find the statue, and he knew the right answer to the clue. Maybe …

I scooted close to Kimo and nudged him. "I believe you. Maile, Sam and I need to try this on our own. But will you stay close to the phone in case we can't find the first one? Would you tell us your answer then?"

A smile overtook Kimo's face. "Okay. I'll stay right here until you call. Then I'll help you." He took a breath. "But you guys have to let me be part of the club after I solve the first clue."

My lips curved to one side. Maile and Sam might kill me if I agreed to Kimo's plan. Our solutions were perfect. My nerdy little brother couldn't possibly have a better one. "Sounds good. You can be an official member."

"Yaaaaaaaay!" He popped off the couch, clapped, and jumped around in a little circle.

"Whoa!" I stuck my palm in his face. "But that doesn't mean you can come with us all the time. This fundraiser is for my school, so I want to find the Menehune statues myself. Of course Maile and Sam will help." I stood up and poked Kimo's arm. "And you will too — but only if you're right about the first answer."

He beamed. "I am."

Shaking my head, I darted out of the house and down the stairs.

Kimo followed me. "Bye. I can't wait for you to call." He zipped back inside before I had a chance to say anything.

My bike and helmet rested against the side of the house. I secured the protective gear on my head, buckled the strap under my chin, and slipped both arms through my backpack straps. Visions of discovering the hidden statue danced in my mind. I climbed onto the bike and pedaled down the driveway onto the street. Pineapple aroma drifted from the fields. Inhaling the sweet scent, I picked up the pace.

Pangs shot through my stomach. Anticipation. And maybe some doubt.

My legs ached as I pushed the bike faster. I worried about being able to surf. My muscles had become weak. I didn't even want to picture my left arm. It would probably be skinny and gross after they removed the cast.

Late summer sunrays spilled through the palms and reflected off the bike's chrome fenders. Soon I was on open road beyond the tall vegetation. Droplets of sweat slid down my face. I knew bike helmets were necessary, but boy, were they hot. I wanted to bat the wet away, but figured it wouldn't be smart. I'd end up steering with only my fingers on my casted left arm which could lead to an unpleasant accident. Didn't need another one of those this summer. One broken arm was enough.

The church and main road to town came into view. I squinted and saw Maile and Sam with their bikes, waiting for me. Grinning, I pushed my legs to power the metal contraption faster.

Maile jumped up and down and waved in wild circles. Sam leaned against his bike, helmet tucked under one arm. I knew they were both into this whole thing as much as me.

Maile's squeal hit my ears. "Hey, Leilani, let's go. Can't wait to track down the first Menehune." She sprayed excitement like a huge wave crashing at Pipeline.

I coasted to a stop. "Give me a minute to rest, okay?"

Sam nodded. "No pro-blem-o. We got here early. Well, 'cause Maile was crazy excited.

"Hey! I know you're excited too." Maile swatted his shoulder. "But because you have to be Mr. Cool-Dude, you won't show it." A grin inched its way across her face. "Don't worry. I won't tell anyone."

He shot a blast of stink-eye at Maile and secured his helmet. "Yeah, well, maybe I am a little, but you and Leilani are way outa control." Sam placed a foot on his pedal. "You ready to go, Leilani?"

"I'm fine." I turned my bike toward town. "Let's go find us a Menehune."

We zoomed down the road. The route was flat all the way. I was glad there were no strenuous climbs. My legs wobbled like Jell-O from all the pedaling.

"Hey, Leilani."

I turned toward Maile's voice.

"Let's stop at the corner by the market. We can walk from there."

"Good idea." Finally. A chance to rest my aching legs.

We parked and locked the bikes. Words erupted from Sam's mouth. "Hurry, guys." He glanced at his watch and tapped a finger on it. "It's almost three. After we walk to Island Games we'll be perfectly on time. 'Course I might starve by then." He dug in his pockets and unearthed a bag of dried mango and some rice candies. "Knew I'd need this stuff." He stuck a handful our direction. "Want some?" He dropped a couple candies in our hands, turned, and marched down the sidewalk. "Time to get on this Menehune thing. Let's go."

Sam wasn't excited one bit. Yeah, right. I shook my head and hollered. "Wait up! We're right behind you." I jogged behind Sam, then slipped in beside him.

Maile fell in next to me. "What happens after we find the statue?"

I unwrapped a candy, but answered before popping it in my mouth. "The instructions said that we have to go to the person in charge of wherever we find it, and tell them where it is. If we're right, the person gives us the second clue."

"Cool." Maile grimaced. "I sure hope the second clue isn't harder than this first one."

I shrugged. "They're all difficult, I'm sure. But we have an advantage."

Talking through a mouthful of dried mango, Sam turned toward me. "We do?"

"Yup. We've already solved a real mystery. This is only a game."

"Island Games ahead." Sam looked at his watch again. "It's like a minute after three o'clock."

Shoulders scrunched to my ears, I smiled. "This is it." I motioned to my friends. "Let's each go a different direction in the store so we cover more area in less time."

"Good idea." Maile marched into the building first and bee-lined it to one of the corners.

"Sam, you take the area opposite from Maile, and I'll look up front."

"No pro-blem-o."

I glanced around the store at the rows of video games and equipment. A concert of beeps, dings, buzzes and electronic music invaded my ears. Kids playing games along the far wall. No use wasting time looking through the aisles of electronics. I hustled toward the sounds, then stopped short.

Just like the clue said, there were plenty of kids and cords. And that was a problem. How could I look for the Menehune? I sucked in a huge breath and stomped forward. I had a mission, and nothing was going to stop me.

"Excuse me." I wedged myself between two kids who were a year or so older than Kimo.

"Hey! What are you doing? You're gonna mess up my game."

"Sorry. I lost something and I need to look for it."

Shaking his head and twisting his mouth, the kid continued to stare forward, pushing buttons on his controller. "Whatever."

I bent and looked around feet and between cords. Nothing. I repeated the routine several more times until I'd thoroughly covered my assigned area. No sign of a Menehune.

"Did you find it?"

I turned toward Maile and shook my head.

"Sam and I didn't find a thing either."

My heart seemed to plummet to my toes. I was so sure the statue would be there. The store fit the clue perfectly. I sighed and pointed to the door. "Let's go to the school. It must be in the computer room."

We raced down the road, Sam in the lead. I panted, my lips and throat drying out with every step. Sam reached the bikes first. He knew the combination for Maile's lock, so he bent down and went to work. Maile and I huffed and puffed our way toward him.

We reached Sam just as he stood, the cable lock dangling from his hand. "Here you are, Maile. Let's get on this. We have to ride all the way to the school."

"Yeah." I sputtered. "Let's go." 'Course I didn't know how I was going to make it without passing out. I sure needed to get back to surfing, otherwise I would turn into a huge slug.

We sped out of town along the main road, passing Heritage Park, Central Community Church, and a few random stores, finally reaching the school. Somewhere along the route I overtook Sam to lead the pack. My legs seemed reenergized. I dropped my bike in front of the school and sprinted inside.

Out of breath, I spit out a few words. "Com ... puter ... room."

"Are you okay?" The young, dark-haired secretary with big glasses narrowed her eyes.

I waved at her and grabbed a breath. "Is it open?"

"Oh. Are you asking about the computer room?"

"Yeah."

She grinned. "Looking for the first Menehune?"

I cocked my head and opened my eyes wide. How did she know? Of course! The Menehune was there and she had the second clue. "Yes." Maile and Sam came to the counter next to me.

"Sorry to disappoint you, kids, but everything except the office is still locked for the summer, so the school computer room is not the right answer to the first clue." Her eyes narrowed. "You're not the only ones to make this mistake. And I bet there'll be more people coming by before the day is over."

"Oh, man!" Sam's shoulders slouched as he dropped into a nearby chair.

Maile joined him. "What do we do now? We don't have another answer to the clue."

I sighed. "I know what we have to do."

"What?"

My friends might totally disown me once I told them. I pulled off my pack, dug for my cell, and clicked it on.

Maile grimaced. "Are you going to tell us or what?"

"I'm calling Kimo."

Ehā
(Four)

"Kimo?" Maile cocked her head.

"I promised him."

Sam stood and dug both hands into his pockets.

I pushed a button and held the phone to my ear. "Sorry, but he told me we were wrong about our answers to the clue, and he knew the right one. So I told him I'd call if we found the statue."

Maile shook her head. "But we didn't find it."

"That's just it." I gulped. "I also said I'd call to get his answer if our two weren't right."

Kimo picked up the receiver and spoke more loudly than needed. "Hey, Leilani! This is Kimo. You didn't find the statue, huh?"

I swallowed hard. "Nope."

"I knew you were wrong. Now I'll tell you the right answer and then you have to let me be a real part of the club."

"Whoa, kiddo. Only if your answer leads us to the Menehune."

"Okay. But I'm right."

Sam motioned for me to follow him outside.

I trotted after him. "We need to hurry, Kimo, so spill it."

"It's at the library in the computer section. Lots of kids go there to play games and stuff."

"What makes you think it's there?"

He snickered. "You didn't read the whole thing."

"Huh? What are you talking about? I studied that stupid clue."

"It says to find and *check him out*. Get it? You check out library books."

My mouth fell open. Kimo was totally right. Every word in a clue was important. Couldn't believe I forgot such a basic rule. What made me think I could be a great detective? I had so much to learn. I missed something my twerpy little brother caught the first time he read it.

Maile nudged me. "Where does he think it is?"

"Talk to you later, Kimo." I closed my cell. "At the library."

She buckled her helmet. "That's a pretty good guess, don't you think?"

Shaking my head, I climbed onto my bike. "It's not a guess. He's right." I took off, pedaling as fast as I could.

"Wait, Leilani." Sam's voice echoed behind me.

I slowed my wild pace and coasted until my two friends caught up.

Sam pulled next to me. "What's with all the crazy pedaling? And why do you think your brother is right?"

"Because I'm a terrible detective."

"What?" Maile coasted along my other side.

I was flanked by the two people who would be most disappointed in me. I'd let them down big-time.

"I don't know what makes you say that, Leilani. You're the best investigator ever. You took the lead in the pineapple case and solved it practically all by yourself."

We turned a corner. The library was four blocks away. "Yeah. But I was pretty worthless with this first clue."

Sam bellowed, swerving his bike almost out of control. "Yeah right, Leilani. You're such a dork. One wrong guess doesn't make you a horrible detective. If Kimo's right, then we'll find the first Menehune and get the second clue. You'll totally do your magic with that one for sure. 'Cause you're way amazing at solving mysteries." He shrugged, stood up on his bike and pressed hard on the pedals. "Bet we'll still be first to find that ole Menehune."

I passed a smile toward Sam's back as he rode ahead.

Maile and I pumped harder to catch up. As we approached the library, Maile pointed. "Let's lock up at the rack in front." She maneuvered her bike onto the sidewalk and coasted to the metal structure.

The gray stone building greeted us with what seemed to be a million steps leading to a huge arching entrance. After making sure everything was locked and secure, we raced up the long stretch of stairs to the front entry.

Sam poked my arm. "Hey! Why's Kimo's answer to the clue better than ours?"

I stopped, dug in my pocket, and pulled out the paper.

"It says, *find and check me out if you can.*" I shook my head. "I should have realized."

Maile shook her head. "I still don't get it."

"You check out books at a library, and lots of kids come and use the computers to play games."

Slapping the railing, Sam grimaced. "Oh, man! Why didn't we see that? Can't believe Kimo figured it out. What is he — like a preschooler?"

I grinned and moved inside. "Let's go."

Our threesome paraded toward the computer area.

There were kids at every station, pounding on keys and moving cursers across the screens. I scanned the area and pointed. "Sam, why don't you start on that end. Maile, you and I will start here. Then we'll meet in the middle."

"Sounds good to me." Sam clomped to the end of the row past a couple adults — probably parents.

I peeked under the first station.

"Hey, what are you doing? You're in my way." A kid about eight years old looked up at me with round blue eyes. Red curls fell across his freckled forehead.

"Sorry. But I need to look under here. Can I scrunch in for just a second?" I could hear a similar conversation happening between Maile and a little dark-haired girl next to me.

"Okay." He scooted aside and I hunkered down. "Whatcha lookin' for?"

I surveyed the equipment and cords under the station. Nothing. "Just making sure everything looks right." I stood. "Thanks."

I glanced at Maile. She shook her head. I spotted a couple of the adults watching us. I ignored them and pushed on.

We moved down the row to the next two stations. Same routine, same conversation with the kids. I got pretty good at sounding official. Staring at the dark mass of electronics under the next computer table, I spotted something. "Yes!" On hands and knees, I moved in for a closer look. Overjoyed, I shook. The plump Menehune statue stared at me, its eyes bright and mischievous. I hoped that we were the first to find it, but the rules said the people who would give us the next clue couldn't tell us how many people had already located the statue.

I backed out and smacked into Maile's feet and legs.

She stepped backward and reached a hand to help me up. "Did you find it? I'm thinking you did since you made that little holler."

I pulled on Maile's hand, stood, and noticed Sam marching toward us, his face sporting a tiny smile. My little hoot must have been louder than I thought.

Maile wiggled as if about to explode from pent-up excitement. "So, what do we do now?"

"On to the second clue." I pointed. But before trekking to the front counter, I made note of the number on the computer station.

The librarian with a round face and frizzy gray hair stared at me. "Do you have books to check out?"

"No. I slipped a hand in my pocket and unearthed the official contest sheet. It proved we were paid up competitors and kept a record of our discoveries. "We just found the first Menehune. It's under computer station number four."

She smiled. "Good job, kids." She stamped the first box. It left the imprint of a chubby Menehune. After scribbling the date underneath, she opened a drawer and pulled out a small piece of paper. "Here's your second clue. Now you know that you're only allowed one find per day, right?"

I nodded.

"Good. Have fun."

My hands shook as I brought the words into focus.

Sam and Maile wedged against me like I was meat between two slices of bread. They spoke at the same time. "What is it? What does it say?"

I giggled at their enthusiasm. "Okay." Clearing my throat, I held the paper up and read it like a TV reporter.

I'm Menehune Number Two.
You might get stuck this time. But don't go off the chart to find me.

Maile wrinkled her nose and twisted her lips. "Man, this one's even weirder than the first clue."

"That's insane. How we gonna figure out this one?" Sam grabbed the paper and held it close to his face as if he might see something more than just the words.

"Don't know." I looked at the wall clock. "It's getting late. Probably should get home. We can think about this clue and call each other tonight with some ideas."

"I'm up for that." Sam headed outside. "Hey!" He rummaged in his pocket and pulled out a metallic blue cell phone. "Cool huh?" His lips curved into a smile.

"I can't believe you just now told us." I narrowed my eyes. "Figured you'd be waving the thing around and texting every friend you know."

He shrugged. "Kinda got into the whole Menehune Hunt thing." His smile faded as he stopped near our bikes. "What happened with your phone, Maile? Your mom ever let you get a new one after you killed your other one?"

"Yup." She pulled a small cell with a bright green cover out of her pocket.

I raised my eyebrows and searched for the right words. "Nice color."

Sam made no attempt to hide his feelings. He burst into laughter. "Looks like a big ole pickle."

Maile sent a sneer his direction. "Hey, I like green."

Sam shook his head and reached for his helmet.

"My mom thinks I should have a cover to protect it. Maybe next time the stupid thing has an accident it won't end up in a billion pieces."

"They didn't have any other colors?" I reached for my helmet, but a voice from behind distracted me.

"Hey, wot's da haps, little sistah?" Maile's older brother, Kainoa, and his friend, Tyler Chin, jogged toward us. The two sixteen-year-olds had been best buddies since preschool, which was funny since they were almost complete opposites. Tyler sported black hair against a backdrop of pale skin and a thin build. He preferred music to water sports.

Kainoa smiled, his sun-drenched hair flopping as he ran. Proof of a great surfing season radiated in his muscles and deep tan.

"Nothing much." Maile answered her brother's question before I could. I was too busy admiring him and his way cool Pidgin English.

"Found the first Menehune yet?"

Maile shrugged. "Maybe." She locked eyes with her brother. "You two still looking?"

"Yup." He turned toward me. "Hey, Leilani."

Hands trembling and clammy, I fumbled with the buckle under my chin. I prayed Kainoa wouldn't notice the shaking. My heart pounded so hard against my chest I was afraid he might hear the thumping. I swallowed hard and forced a smile toward the guy I totally adored. "Hey, Kainoa."

The sounds of children screaming caused our group to turn toward the building. The librarian burst out the door, yelling and waving her hands.

"Fire!"

Elima
(Five)

Kids, adults, and smoke poured out the entrance.

Yelling over his shoulder, Kainoa sprinted toward the building.

"Maile, call 911!"

Maile fumbled with her phone, finally punching in the numbers.

I tossed my bike helmet aside and chased after Kainoa. Sam sprinted up the stairs beside me. I coughed as I inhaled the acrid smoke.

Kainoa grabbed one of the women. "Is anyone still inside?"

She fanned her face. "The librarian went back to check."

"Oh, man!" Lines etched deeply in Kainoa's forehead, and his jaw appeared rigid and determined. He bounded up the last few steps and into the library.

"Kainoa!" I screamed so loud I startled myself with the volume and force. "Don't go in there."

He disappeared into the thick, black fog.

Sam placed a hand on my shoulder. "He'll be okay, Leilani." He pointed toward the street. "There's the fire truck."

I hadn't heard the blaring sirens. Now both the flashing lights and the piercing sound bombarded me.

The trained men and women worked quickly, hooking up hoses and arming themselves with equipment. The adults ushered the kids to a side lawn where they took refuge under palm trees.

Maile approached as Sam and I turned to move out of the way.

A firefighter hauling a huge hose stormed up the stairs. I waved to attract his attention. "There's someone inside."

He turned and hollered. "People inside! Let's move." Then he passed off his load to a co-worker and stepped toward me. "Do you know how many?"

"I'm not sure. At least one sixteen-year-old guy and the lady librarian."

"Thanks." He riveted his eyes on mine. "Now you and your friends need to move away from the area. We'll get everyone out."

I nodded and tried to force a smile as I watched several of the crew, laden with heavy protective clothing and oxygen masks and tanks, enter the building. Clenched hands and white knuckles greeted me when I hung my head to pray.

Dear Lord, protect Kainoa and everyone else in the library.

Maile tugged at my tank top. "Come on, Leilani. We should go."

"Yeah." I plodded down the stairs and toward the bikes.

Tyler was pacing when he spotted us. He waved and yelled. "Everything okay?"

I tried to put on a confident expression.

Maile nudged me. "My brother's going to be fine. He's impulsive and brave, but not stupid."

I nodded.

Sam looked over his shoulder at the thick haze in front of the building. "They'll get everyone out."

Once we reached the bikes, Tyler pelted us with questions. "I can't see a thing over this crowd. Is Kainoa still in there or did they get him out? What about other people?"

Tyler was a caring person. Most guys weren't. Or at least they didn't show it as much as he did. "They made us leave the area." Frowning, I turned my attention to the massive building. I strained to see past all the people and commotion.

Suddenly, movement at the entrance caught my eye. Through the multitude of bodies and thinning smoke I spotted him. Kainoa held a rag over his face and ushered the librarian, a child and another woman outside.

Shrieking, I bolted toward the stairs and shouted. "Kainoa, you okay?"

A policeman stopped me. "You'll have to stay back, miss."

"Sorry." I craned to see around the officers and firefighters. Several grabbed the foursome exiting the building, took them a short distance away, and covered their faces with oxygen masks. I shuddered and wiped an escaping tear off my cheek.

"Is my brother okay?" Maile stood on tiptoe, stretching to see.

Spotting a black streak of wet mascara under her eye, I knew she was scared. "Let's go around the crowd and get closer."

"Sounds like a plan." Sam forged ahead.

"You guys lead on. I'll follow you." Tyler waved us on, then trudged behind.

We maneuvered around the crowd and into the street.

Sam pointed. "There they are."

We picked up the pace and wove around trees and people until finally making it to Kainoa. An officer stepped in front, blocking our path. "Sorry, kids, but you need to be on your way. Everything's okay here."

Maile shook a finger toward Kainoa. "That's my brother."

"I see." He ushered us to the four victims.

Maile fell to her knees next to Kainoa. "You okay?"

He nodded.

"You jerk! You scared us half to death."

He pulled the mask away. "Sorry. I just kind of freaked when someone said the librarian had gone back inside."

Tyler hunkered down next to his friend. "Hey, man. Don't know how smart it was to go into that building. But I do admire your bravery. No one could ever call you a wimp."

Kainoa grinned, then with prodding from an EMT person, he replaced the oxygen mask. His eyes shifted toward me.

Smiling, I knelt. "Can't believe you did that. Scared me big-time!"

His eyes sparkled and little lines appeared around the corners. He'd smiled under the mask.

My heart thundered against my ribs. I swallowed the lump forming in my throat and forced out some words. "Glad you're okay."

The technician leaned over Kainoa, grasped the mask, and pulled it off his face. "You breathing okay without this thing?"

Kainoa raised to a sitting position. "Yeah, I'm good. Thanks."

The EMT guy watched Kainoa for a moment. "You didn't seem to inhale much smoke, but I want you to call a parent so I'm clear that they don't want me to send you to the hospital."

Kainoa followed orders, talked with his mom a moment, then handed the phone to the technician.

Maile touched her brother's shoulder and stood. "Mom say you don't need to go to the hospital?"

"Yeah." He shrugged. "A little freaked at first, but she said I didn't need to go. You know how Mom is — she'll be all over me when I get home. If she thinks anything's wrong, she'll zap me into that hospital bed." He chuckled.

The technician handed the phone to Kainoa. "Okay, son. You're good to go."

Maile pointed toward the bikes. "We're going to ride home now. You coming?"

"Yup. In a few minutes." Kainoa stood and ruffled Maile's hair. "I'll see you there later."

Our threesome trekked toward the bikes. I stared at the huge stone building. Firefighters lumbered out the door while others reeled in the hose. Most people had left the area. I approached one of them as he made his way toward the engine.

Maile and Sam tagged along.

"Excuse me." I stared at the black smears on his face. "Do you know how the fire started?"

He removed his hardhat and shook his head. With a face of stone, he ushered us away. "You kids should move along now. The fire's out and no one was hurt except for a little smoke inhalation."

Not willing to give up on my mission to find out what happened, I motioned for my friends to follow me. We slipped to a corner of the gigantic truck and listened to the conversation between a couple fire fighters.

"Looks like the whole thing started behind some of the bookshelves where a pile of papers caught fire," said an unfamiliar voice.

"Someone was either very careless — or lit it on purpose."

Definitely, this was the guy who sent us away.

"Thank goodness it just mostly smoldered and produced a lot of smoke. Not good with all those people inside," he finished.

I nodded at my friends and motioned for them to retreat.

Once we reached the bikes, Maile worked on the lock.

Sam spewed at least a million words at us. "Can you believe that? What kind of jerk would start a fire in the library? There's always like a b'zillion kids inside. Man, it could have been so much worse than people breathing in a bunch of smoke. Kainoa was crazy to go back inside. Freaked me out big-time."

He stopped for about a millisecond, snatched a quick breath, and passed me a sly grin. "It's cool you're way into Kainoa, and —"

Eono
(Six)

"Whoa!" I stuck my palm in front of Sam's face. "Who says I like Kainoa? I mean, he's nice, but we're just surfing buddies."

He shoved both hands in his pockets and shrugged. "I saw you, Leilani. Your eyes sort of exploded like Fourth of July fireworks." He pointed a finger at me. "And you smiled kinda weird too."

I sighed. "Whatever."

Maile chimed in with her opinion. "Yeah, Leilani. I knew you liked him way back when you first told me about the pineapple vandals."

I set my jaw and shot some lip-curl at my friends. "You two are super pains." I grabbed my helmet and clicked the strap. "Call me tonight and we'll plan tomorrow's search."

Sam poked me. "Didn't mean to make you mad. I won't say anything about this whole crush thing."

I grimaced and clenched my bike's handlebars. "I definitely do not have a crush thing."

I wasn't lying. Kainoa was the love of my life, not some brainless puppy love. Sam didn't understand and Maile just saw him as her surfer-dude brother. "You guys are crazy."

I took off, pedaling as fast as I could. Sam and Maile had seen right through me. Maybe someday I'd tell them the real truth, but for now all they needed to know was that my feelings weren't infatuation.

Tipping my chin upward, I absorbed the tropical warmth. Scents of salty ocean and sweet flowers filled my lungs. The smell of the sea made me long for surfing. I watched the sunlight flicker through palm fronds as I zoomed underneath.

Once my house was only a few blocks away, I slowed my reckless speed and coasted down the slight incline. Scenes from the library played in my mind. Finding the first Menehune. The librarian giving us the second clue. Then the fire. A shiver raced up my back and across my shoulders.

I turned into the driveway and pressed my brakes.

Before I could climb off the bike, Kimo stormed out the front door. "Did you find it?"

"Yup."

Clapping his hands, he jumped up and down. "Way cool! Did you get the second clue?"

"Yup."

"Let me see it. Bet I know the answer. I got the first one right, huh?"

"Hold on, Kimo. Let me get my bike parked." I wheeled it toward the side of the house. "I'll meet you inside, okay?"

Kimo nodded and zoomed up the stairs. He chattered to himself all the way.

Couldn't help but chuckle at the little nerd. I hung my helmet on the handlebar and marched into the house. Dinner smelled wonderful. Teriyaki. Yummy.

"Hello, Leilani." Mom's voice floated from the kitchen. "Was about ready to send out the troops to find you." She stepped through the doorway. "You didn't have an accident again, did you?"

"No, Mom." For some reason this made me giggle.

She waved a wooden spoon at me. "Not funny. You're notorious for having something strange hold you up and make you late."

She was right. "Well, actually …"

Mom planted fists into her sides, the spoon sticking out like a little spout. "Out with it, missy. What happened this time?"

"Not much." I shrugged. "Just a fire in the library."

"Good heavens! You okay? Were you inside when it happened?"

"Everything's okay. But the librarian who'd come out when the fire started, turned right back around and went inside again. Kainoa went after her."

Mom gasped. "Doesn't sound like that was a very smart idea."

"Yeah. But he just reacted. He wasn't in there too long, and he rescued the last three people." I grinned and prayed my mom didn't notice how proud I was of Kainoa.

"That must have been quite the scene."

I nodded. "Maile called 911, so the fire department and police came."

She quick-stepped it across the living room, and grabbed me in a hug. "So glad you or Kainoa or anyone else wasn't hurt." She stepped back and leveled her eyes with mine. "You do know I was kidding about you having accidents or running into strange events?"

I laughed now. "Yeah, right."

Kimo trudged into the room. "What are you doing, Leilani? You ever gonna show me that clue?"

Mom walked toward Kimo, tweaked his nose, then headed into the kitchen. "My fault, kiddo. Sorry."

Kimo danced around me. "Let me see it. I want to figure out the answer."

"Let's go to your room and I'll show it to you."

"Cool." He galloped down the hall and into his room.

I followed behind, plopped onto the bed next to him, and dug in my pocket for the paper. "Here we go." I read the strange clue.

I'm Menehune Number Two.
You might get stuck this time. But don't go off the chart to find me.

Kimo's face looked like a dried prune. "That's kinda weird."

"Sure is." I reached for a pencil on his desk. "Do you have some paper? I'll write this down so you can study it."

"Okay." He rummaged through piles of pads and notebooks and pulled out a half-sheet. "Here."

I scribbled the clue while Kimo gawked over my shoulder.

"Do you have to watch me like that?"

He pointed at the writing. "I can't read it."

"Sorry." I erased the chicken scratch and rewrote the words. "Okay, done. Here you go." Smiling, I handed the paper to my brother. "Your mission is to concentrate on this clue and write down any ideas you have."

Eyes fixed on the message, Kimo nodded. "Okay. But this one is super hard."

"Yeah, well, think about it." I stood and moved toward the door. "I'm sure something will come to you."

Kimo grinned and nodded.

I left his room and plodded down the hall to mine. A little leap and I landed on my bed. It jiggled and squeaked. Planting my head backward into a pillow, I fixed my eyes on the confusing clue. *Stuck.* Maybe it had something to do with glue. I stared some more. People used thumbtacks to stick things on bulletin boards. *Chart.* Teachers used charts, glue and corkboards. Could be a classroom — except the school wasn't open yet, so that wasn't the answer.

I sighed and glanced at the posters hanging on the far wall. All surfers riding amazing waves. Someday I'd be just like them and maybe even be on a poster too. I couldn't help but grin at the image.

Before I could come up with another idea, my thoughts were interrupted by Mom's voice, calling that dinner was ready.

Kimo skipped his way to the kitchen while I followed.

I breathed in sweet teriyaki aroma. "Mmm. Smells great."

Smiling, Mom nodded. "Can you get the rice, sweetie?"

"Sure." I snatched the bowl and placed it on the table.

Once we settled into our seats, Mom said grace and passed the food. "So, did you, Maile and Sam find the first Menehune?"

"Yup. It was in the library under the computer stations."

A huge grin spread across Kimo's teriyaki-smeared face. "And I figured out the clue. Leilani and her friends were way wrong." He laughed. "They rode their bikes all over trying to find it. But I knew the real place."

"Good for you. What's next?" She took in a huge bite of meat and rice.

I chugged some milk and then wiped my mouth. "We go after the second one tomorrow."

"And I'll probably know the right answer 'cause Leilani and her friends aren't good at the clue stuff."

My annoying brother deserved a dose of foul-face.

He stuck out his tongue.

"Okay, you two." Mom waved her fork back and forth between us. "You both have a great talent for this sleuthing stuff. You'd better learn to work together and appreciate each other's skills."

Kimo stared at me with big eyes that seemed to beg for support.

Cocking my head, I forced a grin.

Mom placed the fork on her plate. "Good enough. I'll accept whatever that was as an agreement between you two." She stood. "Now finish up and clear your dishes."

After dinner and clean up I headed to my room and hunkered down with a pad of paper, pen and the clue. Nothing came to mind no matter how long and hard I stared at the crazy thing. Time to check in with Kimo. Maybe he was right. It seemed that I couldn't see the answer no matter how hard I tried.

I tossed the papers onto the bed and headed for the door, but the musical tone of my cell interrupted my trek. I snatched it and glanced at the screen. Maile's home number.

"What's up?"

"Hey, Leilani." The deep voice startled me. "It's Kainoa."

Ehiku
(Seven)

Why was Kainoa calling me? Opening my mouth I prayed the words wouldn't come out in stutters. "Hey. What's up?" Good. I made it through without totally humiliating myself.

"Maile said I should call you."

Maile? I shuddered as panic seemed to overtake my whole body. If she'd said something to her brother about me having a crush on him, I would die right here in my room with my cell phone still at my ear. Swallowing the lump in my throat, I tried to say something.

But he continued. "She said you'd be totally interested in what happened today after you three left."

The phone bounced against my ear as my hand shook. "Something with the fire?"

"Not really, but kind of. The police and firefighters let the librarian back inside the building to check out the damage and get some things she'd left."

"Do you know if it was bad in there?"

"I waited for her and an officer to come out. She told me things weren't too badly burned, except in the back where the fire started. Mostly there was just a whole lot of smoke."

"That's good, right?"

"Guess so. But the library will still have to be closed for a day or so to clean up the mess."

I sighed. "Bummer."

Kainoa didn't say anything. My stomach churned. Then I heard him take in a breath. "That's not the big news."

My already agitated insides raged as if in battle. "Oh?"

"Seems while the librarian was shutting down all the computers she noticed the Menehune was missing."

"What? We found that statue right before the fire started."

"I knew when she said three kids had just found number one, it was you, my sister and Sam." He stammered. "I-I don't know how to say this."

"Oh man! She thinks we took it?"

"Yeah. But that's not the worst part."

My friends and I accused of being thieves. Nothing could possibly be worse than that. I gulped hard. No sound came through the phone line. "Kainoa?"

"The police took down your information. They'll be coming to talk with you."

"Do they think we took it or know something?"

"Yeah …" His voice trailed off.

Tension seemed to ooze from the phone. I sat on my bed and focused on the wood floor.

"I don't know any details because the officers don't share that stuff." He sighed. "I figured you'd like to have a little warning before the police showed up at your house."

"Thanks, Kainoa."

"The police already came to our house, and will be going to Sam's too."

"Does he know?"

"Yeah. Maile called him."

I wished I could be excited about Kainoa calling me, but my mind spun with visions of the computer stations, finding the Menehune, what the librarian thought, and the smoke pouring from the building. There was no room in my head for joy or celebration.

After goodbyes, I shut my phone. Mom was going to be really upset when officers showed up at our house. Maybe not like when they came to tell her about Dad's accident, but it would be bad. I stood and tried to muster up some confidence.

Kimo suddenly darted into my room. "Did you figure out the clue yet?"

I shook my head and covered my face with both hands.

"What's the matter, Leilani?" Kimo tapped my arm.

"Did I invite you in?" I glared at him through watery eyes."

"Uh-uh."

A tear escaped and dribbled down my cheek. I batted it away.

"Man, Leilani. What did you do?"

I forced a tiny smile. "I didn't do anything. It's just …"

"What? I heard your cell a while ago. Did one of your friends get hurt or something?"

I shook my head. "It's kind of hard to explain."

Kimo's little hands were balled into fists at his sides. He glared. "I always have to tell you that I'm smart. I'll understand if you tell me."

I grabbed him by the shoulders, bent low, and riveted my eyes on his. "You can't say anything to Mom, okay?"

"Why?"

"Because I should tell her, not you. Got it?"

He rocked on his feet side to side. "I guess."

"Something happened at the library today." I twisted my

mouth to one side. "There was a fire."

"Wow! Did the firemen come?" Kimo waved his arms in big circles above his head. "Were there lots of sirens and flashing lights? It's so cool when the huge truck goes zooming down the road."

"Yes, they came. But it wasn't very exciting. It was really scary."

"Did you see big flames? Did the whole library burn down?"

I shook my head. "Nope. I didn't see any flames, and the building is still standing. It was mostly just smoke."

Kimo scrunched his nose. "Why don't you want Mom to know about the fire?"

"She already knows about the fire." Rubbing my head I prayed I was making the right move letting Kimo in on the whole story. He'd know soon anyway. "Maile, Sam and I were the last people to find the Menehune before the fire started."

He cocked his head. "How come you know that?"

I spilled the whole story, including the phone call from Kainoa.

"Way cool!"

"It's not cool. I have to talk to the police like I was a criminal or something. And it'll be horrible for Mom, just like before." The scene passed in front of my eyes of Mom sobbing and collapsing when the police came to tell us about Dad.

Kimo hung his head and spoke to his toes. "Yeah. Hope she doesn't cry lots and lots like that again."

I wrapped my arm around his shoulders and squeezed. "Why don't you come with me? We'll tell Mom together, okay?"

He nodded then tipped his head up and gazed at me. "I know you wouldn't take that ole statue. Why would you want it anyway?"

"Yeah, but I don't know what the police think." I squeezed my brother's shoulders again.

"You're squashing me, Leilani."

"Sorry." I loosened my vice grip.

"Maybe they think you tried to ruin the Menehune Hunt so you could win the race."

Before I could say anything about Kimo's theory, the doorbell rang. I cringed.

My brother's eyes grew large. "Is that the police?"

I grabbed Kimo's arm. "Let's go see."

We hustled down the hall and into the living room.

Mom stood at the door. The person she faced was a tall man dressed in a suit. He looked official. Maybe a detective.

Fear wrenched my insides.

"Come in, please." Mom motioned for the two men to enter. As she turned, she spotted me.

I tried to smile, but I couldn't manage it.

Mom's face paled as she turned her attention to the two men.

Now I was sure they were police detectives. Not the kind of visitors I wanted.

"Please have a seat." Mom motioned toward the sofa and then turned a line-creased face toward me. "This is my daughter." She lowered her chin. "Leilani, these police detectives are here to talk with you."

I took several steps on noodle legs. Avoiding her piercing stare, I focused on the official looking men.

"Leilani?" Mom's voice rang stern.

I glanced at her and opened my mouth. Nothing came out.

"Did you have something to do with the fire at the library?"

Ewalu
(Eight)

"No, Mom." I gulped. "I'd never do anything like that."

One of the men stood. "Leilani, why don't you have a seat." He motioned toward a chair.

I nodded and sat.

Mom moved behind me and placed her hands on my shoulders.

"I'm Detective Ray Morris." He tipped his head. "And this guy is my partner, Detective Mike Yamada." Both men seemed super official in their suits, ties and nice haircuts.

When Detective Morris smiled, a calming sensation flowed through my body. My hands stopped shaking, but I still clutched a fistful of my tank top, and squeaked out a few lame words. "Hi. Nice to meet you." No, it wasn't nice to meet them. They were going to accuse me of taking the Menehune, or even worse, starting the fire.

Mom motioned toward the kitchen. "Can I get either of you some coffee or lemonade?"

Detective Morris nodded. "Ice water would be great."

"Nothing for me." Detective Yamada was younger than his partner, but seemed more uptight. He pressed his lips together and stared at me with narrowed eyes.

Detective Morris talked with Kimo who seemed thrilled to tell him stories about summer school, bike riding and playing the ukulele.

Mom walked into the living room and placed a glass of ice-water on a coaster near the detective. "Kimo, I think you should go to your room and read."

"Aw, man! I always miss out on everything." He clomped down the hall, mumbling the entire way.

Detective Morris motioned. "Mrs. Akamai, why don't you have a seat near your daughter? We're going to ask Leilani some questions about the events at the library today." He nodded toward his partner. "I'm letting Detective Yamada take the lead on the interview." He passed the younger man a quick smile. Was he in training or something?

Detective Yamada shot a quick sparking glance at his partner. He pulled a notepad and pen from his jacket. After flipping through several pages, he stopped, and scowled at whatever was written. The more pages he turned, the deeper the lines etched into his face.

I shuddered.

"Miss Akamai, you and your friends, Maile Onakea and Sam Bennett are involved in a fundraiser for the school — The Menehune Hunt, correct?"

I nodded.

"Were the three of you at the library today around 4:00?"

"Yeah. Maybe a little after. I'm not sure."

"Were you there to look for the Menehune statue?"

"Yes, sir."

"Did you find it?"

I squirmed, then nodded. "Under one of the computer stations."

He looked up from the notebook and tapped the pen on his chin. "What did you do after you located it?"

My palms turned wet. I wiped the right one on my shorts. Nothing I could do about the left one imprisoned in the cast. "We checked in with the library lady and got the second clue."

"And then?"

I shrugged. "We went outside to get our bikes and leave."

Detective Yamada cocked his head. His stare seemed to pierce right through my chest. "But you were there when the fire started around four-forty, right?"

"Yes."

He waved the pen around. "What were you doing between the time you found the statue and the time the fire started?"

I swallowed hard to stop a groan. "We read the clue and talked about it for awhile. Then we went to our bikes to go home, but Maile's brother, Kainoa, and his friend, Tyler, came by." I swallowed hard. "So we talked with them until the library lady came out yelling."

"Okay." He scribbled something in the notebook. "Did you and your friends see anyone around the computer stations who seemed like they didn't belong? Or someone acting strange?"

"Someone acting strange?"

"Yeah, like an adult watching kids at the computers who didn't appear to be a parent. Or maybe someone wandering around, but not actually looking for a book."

I closed my eyes and pictured the inside of the library. I knew there were adults there today, but I couldn't see them. Shaking my head, I opened my eyes. "Sorry. I was so into finding the statue I can't picture anyone but the kids at the computers."

Detective Morris smiled and shook his head. "Don't worry about it, Leilani."

Tears blurred my vision. I prayed they wouldn't spill. "Do you think I started the fire and took the Menehune?"

Mom gasped and covered her mouth with both hands.

"I'm sorry we scared you." Detective Morris stood. He took a step toward me, bent, and placed a hand on my shoulder. "After talking with you three kids and the older brother, I really don't think any of you were involved." He sighed and stood up straight. "But someone started that fire."

"Do you think the same person took the Menehune?"

He shrugged. "Could be. Seems to make sense the fire was started as a diversion. But we're looking at every possibility." He focused on my mom and stuck out his hand. "Thank you, Mrs. Akamai. I'm sorry we alarmed you when we showed up."

"It's okay." She grasped his hand. "Just brought back some unpleasant memories."

"Now, Leilani, I want you to do something for me." He locked his eyes on mine. "Think about the scene in the library some more, and if you come up with anything, please call, okay?" He handed me a card.

Mom walked outside to the lanai with the detectives. After they left, she moved inside, closed the front door, and leaned her back against it. Wet streaks glistened on her cheeks.

"Mom?"

She wiped the moisture away. "Sorry."

"I was going to tell you the police were coming, but Kainoa called to tell me right before they showed up."

She shuffled across the floor and wrapped both arms around me. "I know. None of this is your fault." She placed a finger under my chin and tipped my head. "I feel bad I immediately assumed the worst about you. Guess I went a little crazy when the detectives said they needed to talk with you about the incidents at the library." She sighed. "I also relived the time when the police showed up —"

"It's okay, Mom."

She smiled and squeezed me tight. "I love you, sweetie. It's just so hard to cope sometimes without your dad around."

Before I had the chance to say anything, Kimo skipped down the hall, across the room, and plowed into us. He giggled. "You love me, too, right? 'Cause I love you, Mom."

She smiled. "Yes I do, very much."

"I can do some things like Dad. Wouldn't that be good?"

She ran fingers through his hair. "You're so sweet."

Kimo, sweet? Not the words I'd choose to describe him. Irritating and dorky. Much better description.

After the great group hug, Mom headed into the kitchen. "I'm thinking I could use a cupcake right now. How about you two?"

Kimo jumped up and down and clapped madly. "Yaaaaaa-aaaaay! I love cupcakes. Make chocolate ones with lots of white frosting and sprinkles."

Mom chuckled. She pulled the cupcake tins from a drawer. "Why don't you both go do whatever and I'll call you when they're ready?"

I started down the hall, then yelled at her. "Lots of sprinkles, Mom. I love them too, especially the cinnamon ones."

I heard Mom laugh.

"Leilani, can we figure out the clue?" Kimo scampered in a circle around me.

"Yes, we'll work on it." I was as anxious as my brother to find the next statue. But something else played over and over in my mind. The missing Menehune. And the fire.

"I'll get the little paper you gave me." Kimo took off.

As I passed his open door, I stuck my head in. "Meet me in my room."

Once in my safe haven, I sat on the floor and hung my head. My hands still shook a little. I couldn't figure out why anyone would want to start a fire in the library. Like the detective said, it could have been part of a master plan to create a diversion and steal the Menehune. But why? It was just an ugly statue.

"I got it, Leilani." Kimo dropped down next to me and slapped the paper on the floor.

"Good." I sighed. "Have any ideas?"

"I keep thinking and thinking …"

"All I could come up with was a classroom because of all the glue and charts. Except my school isn't open yet."

Kimo's eyes opened wide. "But mine is. That's where I'm taking stupid math at summer school."

"You could be right." I stared at the clue. "But let's see if we can come up with something else just in case that's not it."

He shrugged. "Okay."

But I couldn't think about the answer. A little movie of the library played in my mind. I willed myself to focus on the scene. Who else was around the area?

"I can't think of anything else."

Kimo's voice distracted me from the vision. I blinked and refocused on him. "That's okay. Why don't you check your classroom tomorrow?"

He nodded.

"Is anything else besides your math classroom open right now?"

"I think so."

"If you don't find it in your room, do you think you could check the others?"

He shrugged. "Guess so. I'm real good at finding things."

"Hey!" Mom yelled down the hall. "Cupcakes are ready."

"Hooray!" Kimo leapt to his feet.

I followed him to the kitchen.

"I haven't frosted them. Figured you'd like to do that yourselves and put on whatever sprinkles you want." She handed us each a knife and pointed at the table with the fresh baked treats, a bowl of frosting and several jars of sprinkles.

Kimo dug right in and managed to fling frosting everywhere.

I settled into a chair. Distracted by thoughts of the afternoon's events, I ignored *Project Cupcake*. Snapshots paraded through my mind.

Then I saw it.

Eiwa
(Nine)

Today, at the library, I'd seen a young, dark-haired man, his Mariners' blue baseball cap resting low on his forehead and his head tipping down so I couldn't see his face. Dressed in board shorts, a ragged t-shirt, and a shark's tooth around his neck, the guy fiddled with a metal thing in his hand. He turned it over and over. It caught the overhead lights and glinted. Was it maybe a lighter?

I stood and raced past Mom, out of the kitchen.

"Leilani, what are you doing?"

"I'll be right back." I called to her over my shoulder and continued the mad pace into my room where I grabbed my cell.

Phone in hand I hit the button to call Maile.

"Hey, Leilani. What's up? You figure out the clue?"

"Naw. I mean Kimo has an idea, but that's not why I called."

"Oh. The police, huh? Were you as scared as me? Bet you were much braver."

I waved my hand around. "Yeah — I mean, later. Right now I have something major important to tell you. It's about the library." I swallowed a big breath. "The detectives told me to think about it in case I remembered seeing something." I clenched my teeth and shimmied as excitement built inside. "There was a guy near the computer stations, and I think he had a lighter in his hands."

"For real? Think he's the one who started the fire?"

"Don't know, but it could help the police."

She smacked her lips. "What did he look like? Maybe I saw him too. I remember walking past a couple people in the computer area."

I described the man. "When we started looking around the computer station, I was concentrating so hard, nothing else registered until a few minutes ago."

"Good thing those detectives told you to think about it. You going to call them tomorrow?"

I nodded as though she could see me. "Yeah, but I have to get my cast off in the morning, so I'll call after I'm done."

Maile squealed. "Oh, man! I forgot about that. You excited or what?"

I grinned. "A little."

"Yeah, right. You've only been waiting all summer to get that thing off. When ya gonna hit the beach with your board?"

"As soon as I can."

She giggled. "Call me when you're cast-free, okay?"

After I hung up, I called Sam, explained everything to him, and promised to call again once my arm was out of prison.

I made my way to the kitchen and re-joined the cupcake party. It was late, so I'd call the police tomorrow.

Mom, Kimo and I giggled and made a huge mess.

Kimo sported a frosting-and-sprinkle-plastered smile. Waving his knife around, he laughed. "Remember when Dad made you a birthday cake, Mom?"

She smiled and nodded.

"It was sooooo cool when the top layer slipped off." He howled. "And it almost splatted onto the floor."

Mom chuckled. "Yeah, I remember. Especially the part where I tried to rescue the thing as it avalanched its way toward the ground." She shook her head. "But all I managed to do was squish the cake between every finger."

Kimo spoke through a mouthful of cake and frosting. "You looked so funny, Mom."

She nudged him. "I'm sure I did."

"But the funniest part was when you shook your hands."

"Hey, I was only trying to get the frosting and cake to slide off."

I shook my head. "But, Mom, the gunk flicked all over Dad's face."

Kimo held his belly and barely spit out the words. "H-he looked like an a-alien."

We laughed until tears rolled down our cheeks.

I grabbed my stomach and yelped. "Stop! It hurts."

Once our hysterics calmed, I gobbled two cupcakes loaded with a bunch of colorful sprinkles.

Kimo pointed at me and grinned. "You have so much frosting and topping thingies all over your face. Now you look like something from outer space."

I scowled and shot him some mean-mouth. "Figure I can't look half as bad as you, Mr. Frosting-Face."

He stuck out his chocolate-cake-covered tongue.

"Gross!" I stuck my finger into my open mouth and mimicked a huge gag. "Let's help Mom clean up."

Kimo protested with a loud whine. "But I'm not done yet. These cupcakes are super yummy 'cause I'm such a cool froster."

"Quit being such a baby. You've eaten enough for me, Mom and you combined." I grabbed my dishes.

Mom stood and tweaked his nose. "Sorry, mister. You've had way too many sweets tonight. Time to bring your plate, knife and milk glass to the sink, please."

"Awwwww, Mom." Kimo shook his head, stood, and did what he was told.

I could identify with how my brother felt. It was great to laugh so hard and just enjoy being silly together. There was never a moment when Kimo didn't want some fun and craziness. I needed it too.

And so did Mom.

The next morning I opened my eyes a tiny bit and reached for my chiming phone alarm. As I rolled over and groaned, I realized what the early wake-up meant. My cast was finally coming off.

I flung the covers aside and bolted into the bathroom. I mentally outlined my day. First, I'd get free of my gross cast. Second, I'd call Detective Morris about the person I'd seen at the library. Third, I'd check in with Kimo about the second Menehune. And fourth, if we were right about it being in a classroom at his summer school, we'd work on the third clue. I grinned.

Securing my hair into a ponytail, I trekked down the hall and into the kitchen. I never would have known it had been a major mess the night before.

"Good morning, sweetie." Mom pulled a carton of milk from the fridge and carried it and a box of cereal to the table. "We need to move quickly today in order to get Kimo to school and you to the clinic, so it's plain old cereal for breakfast."

I giggled. "You know granola is my favorite."

"Yeah, well, convince your brother to like it too, okay?" She winked. "Excited about this morning?"

"Oh, man! Totally! I keep imagining myself on my board, catching the most amazing wave ever. Can't wait."

"Just be careful, okay?" She handed me a napkin while I poured a glass of milk. "You haven't been surfing all summer, so you may be a little rusty."

I shrugged. "Maybe. But I plan to make up for every moment I missed."

Kimo trudged into the kitchen and plopped onto a chair. He scowled.

"Hey." I nudged him. "Summer school's almost over, right?"

He shrugged, poured milk over his cereal, and played with the spoon.

"Don't forget the mission." I leaned in close and whispered in his ear. "You've got to check the classrooms for the second Menehune statue."

He cocked his head and seemed to perk up a bit. "Oh, yeah. That'll be way cool when I find it, huh?" He plowed into the bowl of crunchies and shoveled in bites.

"Yup. I was totally excited when I found number one. Just don't forget to ask about the third clue. Tell the teacher that when Mom and I pick you up I'll have the paper to stamp, okay?"

Kimo's head bopped up and down like a springy jack-in-the-box.

"Five minutes, you two." Mom gathered up the cereal box and milk jug.

Kimo and I swallowed the last several bites and downed our milk. I hustled to my bathroom, brushed my teeth, then darted back into my bedroom and grabbed my cell.

As usual, my pain-in-the-pants brother made the whole thing a race. Even though I charged out of my room first, he ran from behind, nearly knocking me over as he rounded in front. "Kimo! You little twit." I picked up the pace as I bee-lined it across the living room to the pile of flip-flops.

At the front entry we shoved toes into slippers and blasted out the screen door onto the lanai.

Mom shook her head as we galloped down the stairs and slammed into the side of the SUV. "Why is everything a competition with you two?"

"Ask Kimo. He's the one who always starts it."

"Uh-uhh." He contorted his face and flashed me a silly look.

"You don't have to follow, Leilani." Mom waved her hands. "Let's go."

After securing the seatbelt I closed my eyes and pictured myself riding giant waves on my amazing seven foot longboard. A shiver of excitement curled up my back. The camera in my mind shifted to a second wave. Kainoa rode his board strong and controlled, his sun-streaked hair blowing behind. He twisted to the side and swung his arms for balance. I sighed. Soon the daydream would be true. I loved surfing, and nothing would be better than spending those water hours with Kainoa.

Mom turned into the school parking lot. "Here you go, mister." She turned and smiled at Kimo who sat still in the back, sporting a tight-faced scowl. "Why so sad? Only a couple days left and then you'll be free to romp on the beach and ride your bike."

"Yeah." He unbuckled and slid out of the truck.

I stuck my head out the window and spoke in a low voice. "Don't forget your mission."

His frown morphed into a slight grin. "I won't."

"Talk to you later today."

He nodded and trudged into the building.

Mom slipped the truck into gear. "You're a good big sister."

"Huh?"

"Couldn't help but overhear you say something about a mission." She turned onto the road and headed toward the clinic. "I imagine you're letting Kimo in on some of the Hawaiian Island Detective Club things. Right?"

"Kind of. We really don't do the club stuff anymore." It existed, but for real now, not pretend. Maile, Sam and I solved crimes like the pineapple mystery. And now maybe the whole fire and missing Menehune thing. "Kimo's helping us with the Menehune Hunt."

"You know, he looks up to you, Leilani."

Seriously? I found that hard to believe since he always tried to drive me crazy. I gazed at the passing scenery, eager not only to have my arm freed, but to get the third clue after Kimo found Menehune Number Two.

Mom turned into the clinic lot. "Here we go." She parked. "Excited to get the cast off?"

Excited didn't seem close to the right word to describe how I felt. "Yup." I hustled out of the truck, up the stairs, and into the clinic.

Maggie, the same receptionist from when I broke my arm, looked up from her huge computer screen.

Couldn't help but grin. "I'm here to get this thing off."

"Ahh, yes."

Mom unearthed the medical insurance card and shoved it toward Maggie.

"It will be just a minute." She punched some keys. "You can have a seat."

I followed Mom and sat on a padded chair.

Nervous energy exploded from my body in the form of wiggles and finger tapping.

Mom delivered a stern glance.

"Sorry." I tugged on my shorts and squirmed in my seat. My mind slipped back in time to the day I got my cast and an unexpected tetanus shot ...

I opened my eyes wide. Of course!

I'd solved the clue.

Umi
(Ten)

I got *stuck* with a needle. And there were charts in a doctor's office. The clinic had to be the right answer.

"Come on back, Leilani." The nurse approached, paperwork in hand. She turned toward my mom. "You can wait for your daughter out here if you'd like, Mrs. Akamai. It won't take too long."

Mom nodded. "Have fun."

I followed the nurse, not knowing which I should be more excited about. Getting my uncomfortable, heavy cast off, or finding the second Menehune. I wanted to run through the clinic and check every room, office and closet.

She ushered me into the cast area and helped me onto the table. "The technician will be here shortly."

"Thanks." I sighed. No, the hidden Menehune couldn't be in a private space. Even though the first one hid under a computer table, anyone could get to it. Only patients used exam rooms. I'd probably be in huge trouble if I opened every door and peeked in.

Squeezing my eyes tight, I pictured the clinic. Every public area. My eyes popped open and I smiled. The statue had to be in the waiting room.

"Hello, there, Leilani." The familiar voice caught my attention.

I focused on the young, cute technician scurrying toward me. His red hair was more of a blonde now, longer than when he first put my cast on.

"Hey! It's Dan-The-Cast-Man."

Beaming, he shook his head. "You ready to get that bad boy off?"

"Duh!" I opened my eyes wide and cocked my head.

"Well then, let's get to it." He wheeled a chair close and settled in.

"It's kinda cool you put this thing on and now you get to take it off."

"Oh, didn't I tell you? I live here." He snickered. "And I think you've got it wrong."

I frowned.

"I put your cast on *twice* as I recall." He grabbed a tool that reminded me of a hand mixer, except instead of blades, it had a little round saw on the end.

"Oh, yeah. Forgot about the whole rain disaster." I stared at the evil looking thing in his hand.

Dan smiled. "Don't let this scare you. Remember, we went through this last time. It's designed to cut through plaster only. It can't hurt you."

I nodded. "Okay."

"Hold your arm like this." He demonstrated. The saw buzzed and Dan grasped my cast with one hand and guided the blade with the other.

I liked the vibration and the sound.

Once he broke the plaster away and removed the padding and sock thing, he rested my arm on the table.

"Yes! My arm has finally been paroled from prison."

He passed me a crooked grin. "I'm going to check it out and make sure everything's okay."

"You mean maybe it's not healed and I might still need a cast?"

"Don't panic. It's highly unlikely, but I do need to check for swelling." He touched my arm and ran a couple fingers along the area above my wrist. "If anything seems abnormal, I'll send you to Dr. Lim." He shook his head. "Nope. Nothing wrong. You look good as new."

I stared at my white, scrawny arm and grimaced. "Doesn't look so normal to me."

"Kind of a shocker, huh?" He rolled away on the chair and made notes on a clipboard. "Once you start using it again and get out in the sun, the muscles will come back to normal and your skin will gain color." He wiped away plaster bits. "You take care of this arm, okay? If you're going to be surfing and racing around the island, please be careful."

I nodded. "Believe me. I don't want to come back here again. Not that you're not a nice person —"

He smiled and waved his hand. "Yeah, yeah. I know. You probably have some buff surfer dude waiting on the beach for you right now."

I blushed and shrugged.

"Hmm. So there is a lucky guy hanging out at the shore." He winked.

Kainoa's name must have been etched in my forehead or something. First Sam and now Dan. I sucked in a deep breath.

"Catch a couple big waves for me, okay?" He stood, helped me off the table, and pointed me toward the lobby.

I padded down the hall and into the waiting area. Mom

seemed totally involved in some magazine. Maybe I had time to find the statue. I panned the room, peeked behind a couple plants, and looked under a few chairs before Mom glanced up from her reading.

"Oh, sweetie. I didn't know you were done." She tossed the magazine onto a messy stack. "How's the arm?"

I held it out. "Kind of weird. But better than being in a cast."

"Now I don't want you to rush right out and start surfing, okay? You need to take some time to strengthen your arm."

"But, Mom —"

"No arguments. I'll be right back." She grabbed her purse and headed to the bathroom.

I trudged toward the front counter and observed the area. Computer, clipboards, coffee mug, pens, check-in sheets and a bunch of folders in the corner. An indentation on the top file caught my eye. *Don't go off the chart …*

Of course. The folders were patient charts, and the stack had an impression in the middle, as if the statue had been sitting on it. I leaned against the counter. "Do you have the second Menehune?"

Maggie leveled her eyes with mine. A sly smile spread across her lips. "If you think it's here, you have to tell me where it's hiding before I can give you the third clue."

"I think it should be on that stack of charts." I nodded toward the pile.

Maggie turned. Mouth open, she stared. "Uhh. It was there before I went to the back a few minutes ago." She pushed her chair away from the counter and looked underneath. When her head popped up, she blinked her huge round eyes several times. "It's not on the ground." She stood and plowed through everything on and around the front counter. No Menehune.

"So it was here before you went to the back?"

"Yes. I-I don't understand this. Who would take it and why?"

I shook my head. "Don't know. But did you know the first statue was taken from the library yesterday?"

"Really?" She plopped onto her chair and sighed loudly.

Mom approached, fumbling in her purse, probably looking for the car keys.

"Hey, Mom, did you see anyone come into the clinic and go to the counter while Maggie was gone?"

She twisted her lips. "I don't know. Maybe, but I was so into that article."

"That's okay. Think about it and you can let me know later if you remember anything." I focused on Maggie. "Could I get the third clue?"

"Oh, yes." She rummaged through papers in a drawer. "Here you go. Do you have your check-in sheet?"

I'd remembered at the last minute to stick the thing in my pocket. Figured I might need it if Kimo had found the Menehune in one of the classrooms. I pulled it out and shoved the paper at Maggie.

She stamped and dated it. "Do you think the two missing statues are connected?"

"Could be." For sure they were. The Menehune Hunt game had morphed into a real mystery. Time for me, Maile and Sam to use our detective skills to figure it out. Butterflies took wing in my stomach. I couldn't wait to tell my friends. Two statues missing and they needed rescuing for real.

Mom finally unearthed the keys. She glanced at Maggie. "Thanks. Hope I don't see you anytime too soon." She smiled, turned, and plodded out the door.

Clenching the third clue, I trotted behind her. Ideas whirled in my mind. Suspects, motives and clues.

Surprised my left arm worked so well, I hoisted myself into the truck and buckled up.

The engine roared when Mom turned the key. "Strange how two of those little statues are missing."

"More than missing, Mom. Stolen."

She nodded. "Right." Maneuvering the huge SUV out of the parking spot, she sighed. "Have you read the third clue?"

"Not yet. I've been too busy trying to figure out what's going on."

"Maybe you should see if you can locate that one. It could be missing too."

"Yeah." I uncrumpled the paper, but before I could read the words, Mom yelped.

"Oh! I think I remember something from the clinic."

"You do?"

"Yes. It was a guy who came in. I looked up from the magazine for only a moment as he walked up to the counter." She drew in air. "The next thing I remember is hearing the front door shut. I thought how strange for someone to come in and then leave immediately."

"Do you remember anything about him?"

She shook her head. "Not much. I only saw him from the back. His hair was dark and he was wearing a baseball cap. He could have been Asian. The main thing I remember was the Seattle Mariners' jersey."

Umikumakahi
(Eleven)

"A Mariners' Jersey? The cap too?"

Mom tilted her head to one side. "Could have been. But I only saw him from the back."

"Do you remember the cap's color?"

"Kind of a royal blue I think." She narrowed her eyes. "Are you thinking that he's the thief?"

I sighed loudly. "Don't know." My friends and I needed to meet and make an investigation plan. Hands shaking, my body suddenly filled with energy and excitement. A grin slid across my lips. The second mystery of the summer. How amazing was that?

Mom stopped the truck in front of Kimo's school. "We're a little early. It'll be a few minutes before Kimo comes out."

My brother would take longer than a few minutes. He always messed around before getting to what he was supposed to be doing. And today he'd probably be running from room to room to look for the hidden Menehune. "Can I go inside and meet him?"

She pulled her eyebrows together and cocked her head. "You *want* to get your brother?"

I shrugged. "Maybe I can push him to move a little faster."

Mom chuckled. "Good luck. It's room one-twenty-one."

I hustled out of the truck, into the school, and down the hall to Kimo's classroom. I dug into my pocket, unearthed my cell as I ran, and punched the quick-dial button for Maile.

"Leilani! Your cast off yet?"

"Yeah, but that's not important."

"Yeah, right. Like I believe you."

"Really. You, Sam and I have to meet today." I swallowed hard. "I found the second Menehune."

"Oh, man! Why didn't you wait for me and Sam?"

"It was by accident. I mean, I figured out the clue while I was at the clinic because it all made sense."

"That crazy thing made sense?"

"Yup. Remember when I broke my arm?"

"Duh."

"I had to get a tetanus shot." I grabbed a breath. "So, I got *stuck*. Get it?"

"Cool. I mean, not because of the shot, but —"

"I know. Anyway, the part about not going off the chart meant the Menehune was on a chart."

"Wow!"

I puffed out my chest. Not that it mattered. No one was around to see my silly pride ... *Sorry, God.* I was really going to need His help now that the Menehune Hunt had become a real-life crime. "But that's not the best part."

"Huh?"

"I saw the imprint of where the statue had been sitting, but it was gone."

"Gone? Like stolen?"

"Yup."

Maile stayed quiet for a moment. "Okay. So, here's what we'll do. I'll call Sam and tell him everything. You two can come over here and we'll get started on the whole detective thing. Maybe I'll even fix some lunch." She snickered. "Investigators need their energy, you know."

I set my jaw. "Perfect. I'll get there as fast as I can. Right now we're picking up Kimo from school."

"Oh, I almost forgot. Did you get the third clue?"

"Uh-huh." Staring at my empty hand, I realized I'd left it in the SUV. "I mean, I got it, but it's in the car. We'll go over it when I get to your house."

I pocketed my phone and popped up and down, a little squeal escaping my mouth. Totally dorky, but I couldn't help being major excited about our investigation. But before I could plan anything, the classroom door opened and a bunch of noisy kids streamed past me.

Rising on tiptoes, I surveyed the crowd. No Kimo. Then I caught a glimpse of him wandering around the room. I made my way through the maze of desks and chairs.

"Hey, Kimo, let's go."

He stared at me, then he squinted and pursed his lips. "Why are you here? I'm still looking for the little statue."

I snatched his backpack. "And you're doing a great job, but we've got to go."

His voice transformed into a whine. "How come? I want to find it, Leilani."

"I already found it." Motioning for him to follow, I plodded toward the door.

He stomped behind me. "How'd you do that?"

"It was in the clinic."

Silence.

I trekked down the hall, Kimo lagging behind. Then,

suddenly he bulleted after me. "Cool! I get it. That's so funny." He belly laughed. "You got stuck with a needle, right? And there are lots of charts at the doctor's."

"Good job, Kimo." I grinned.

"Where's the third clue? I can figure it out."

I shook my head. "It's in the car. You can look at it, but I'm going to Maile's house. Sam's coming, too, and we're going to work on solving it."

"Can't I come?"

"No, Kimo. This thing has changed. It's not just the Menehune Hunt game anymore."

"Huh?"

"It's a real mystery now." I jogged to the big truck and opened the door.

Kimo jumped in the back and I flung his pack onto the seat next to him. "I don't get it. How come it's a real mystery now?"

Sighing, I climbed into the front seat. "Because two statues have been stolen."

"The one at the doctor's is gone too?"

"Yup."

Mom slipped the truck into gear and drove toward home. "Oh, Mom, could you drop me at Maile's?"

She gave me a quick sideways glance. "Are you and your friends going to get involved in this whole mess?"

I shrugged. Mom hadn't been too happy when she found out I'd been involved in the pineapple vandalism mystery. Actually, she kind of freaked. Better for me not to make this a big deal. "Not really. But we do have a third clue. Probably should try to figure it out."

She sighed. "All right, but no playing the hero, okay?"

I nodded, knowing I would get more involved than she

wanted. But a hero? I'd never considered myself a hero, so it was okay to agree. Sporting a stern don't-you-say-a-word face, I glared at Kimo in the back seat. Mom never found out about the secrets Kimo knew from the pineapple investigation. And I was sure that Kimo would blackmail me forever with them.

He returned a sly grin. "Leilani says I can help figure out the next clue and find the third Menehune."

Mom glanced in the rearview mirror. "Oh, she did, huh?"

Kimo nodded like a bobble-head gone crazy.

"Well, mister. Your help will just have to wait."

"Mahhhhhm! How come?"

She turned into Maile's driveway. "Summer school is almost over."

"Uh-huh. So that means I can help Leilani and her friends."

"No." Mom put the car into park and turned toward Kimo.

He stared at her with big, sad puppy dog eyes.

"We have a final conference with your teacher this afternoon."

ʻUmikumālua
(Twelve)

Kimo thumped backward into the seat. "Ah, man!" He scowled.

Mom saved my day. I didn't want my annoying brother tagging along. But something tugged at my heart. He'd really helped us with the pineapple mystery. Maybe Maile, Sam and I could figure out something for him to do.

Mom smiled, reached back, and touched his leg. "You've done a great job, kiddo."

Silence.

She cocked her head. "Tell you what. How about you and I go on a date after we meet with your teacher?"

A little smile sneaked through the sour look. "Shave ice?"

"Of course. I'll even let you have the giant one."

Kimo bounced. "Cool!"

I grinned. "Have fun, Kimo." I reached toward him. "Give me a piece of paper and a pencil. I'll write down the third clue so you can work on it."

He dug in his bag and handed me what I needed. I read the clue, then copied it. The crazy thing stumped me. Maybe worse than the last. At least I'd have Maile and Sam to help me decipher. "Here ya go."

Kimo snatched the paper and glued his eyes on the words. "Call me if you figure it out."

No sound from my brother. Did he hear me?

"'Cause you're really smart and you know things." I used my best ten-year-old-Kimo voice, but he seemed totally absorbed, unaware of my way cool imitation.

"Yup. I do."

Frowning at my brother, I shoved his leg. "You little rat. You did hear me."

He waved me off, still focused on the paper. "I'll figure it out. Bye."

I shook my head, opened the door and slid out of the truck.

Mom leaned across the front seat. "Let me know when you're ready to go home and I'll come get you."

"Thanks, Mom. Maile's going to fix lunch, so we'll probably just hang out all day." I shut the door and waved.

Once I reached the lanai of the Onakea home, I climbed the stairs and knocked on the door. Couldn't wait to show off my newly freed arm to my friends, and to share the new clue.

Before I could come up with a list of things the three of us needed to do, Maile opened the door and grabbed me. "Come on, Leilani. Sam's here and we're waiting to start planning the investigation."

A bolt of excitement streaked through my body as I remembered what Mom said about the guy in the clinic, and how maybe it was the same person I'd seen at the library.

Maile dragged me down the hallway and into her room. I loved all the white whicker furniture. But my favorite thing was the red and white Hawaiian quilt draped across her bed. The curtains danced around as a gentle, flower-scented breeze blew through the open window.

Sam jumped up from Maile's desk and trucked toward me, waving a finger at my arm. "Let's see it. Bet it feels weird, huh? Like all naked and gross?"

While Sam paused for a quick breath, I held out my arm.

"Whoa! It's so wimpy and white. Kinda yucko. What's it like? Did it —"

"Stop!" I stuck a palm in his face. "I'm fine, Sam. The technician at the clinic told me my arm will look better once I start using it. Something about the muscles in my arm had atrophied — I think that's the right word."

"Oh yeah. Heard that before." He shifted his stare from my arm to my eyes. "So Maile said you have lots to tell us. Something about a plan, like maybe there's a real mystery going on? Spill it."

"Yup." I plopped onto the bed and placed the paper with the clue in front of me. Slapping a hand on it, I grinned at my friends. "Here's the third one."

The two of them settled in next to me, atop the bright quilt.

Sam stretched out, sunk an elbow into the bedding, and propped his head. "Before you read, what's up with the second Menehune?"

"Okay." I related the entire crazy story, even though I was pretty sure Maile had already filled Sam in on all the details. "Oh, you guys, here's the best part." I took in a long, full breath. "When the police came over last night they asked me to think about who and what I'd seen at the library while we were searching for the statue. Did they ask you two the same thing?"

"Yup." Sam nodded and Maile joined him.

"Later on last night I remembered something."

Maile jumped in before I could describe what I saw. "The dark-haired guy with the Mariners' cap, shark's tooth necklace,

Hawaiian shorts and the lighter?"

"Yeah." I leaned in close. "After Mom and I left the clinic this morning, she suddenly remembered a man who came into the clinic while the receptionist was in the back. He walked to the counter, but then left right away."

Sam sat up and pulled a candy bar from his pocket. "Did she see him take the Menehune?"

I shrugged. "She was busy reading, so didn't really pay too much attention." I raised my eyebrows. "But, she did remember a little about him."

"Oh, man!" Maile sat upright. "Was it the same guy?"

"Don't know for sure, but my mom said he had dark hair, wore a blue cap, and had on a Mariners' baseball jersey."

"Wow! So you're thinking it could be the library person? And he stole both statues?"

Nodding, I swallowed hard. "So now it's a mystery instead of a fundraiser. A for real crime."

Sam spoke sticky words through a mouthful of chocolate and caramel. "We need to get on this missing Menehune thing. Leilani, are you gonna write a list of suspects and motives?" He tore the wrapper on a candy bar and took a large bite. "Hey, we should have another stakeout. But not like the last one. Creeped me out." He swallowed and wiped a hand across his mouth. "Think Kimo's up for helping us?"

Maile rolled her eyes and shook her head. "Sam, You're the grossest person ever when you eat and talk at the same time."

He shrugged. "Can't help it. I'm always hungry and I have lots to say."

Maile sneered at him and opened a drawer. She gathered a pad of paper and a pencil and handed them to me. "Lets start taking notes."

"You take them, Maile." I wagged a finger at the pad. "First, we need to figure out a motive. Second, make a list of possible suspects."

"Okay." She pointed the pencil at me. "Let's start here. What could be some motives?"

Sam wadded the wrapper and tossed it into the trashcan near Maile's nightstand. "Someone wants to wreck the fundraiser big-time."

"Good." Maile scribbled on the pad. "That would mean anyone who hated the school would be a suspect."

"Like maybe a student or a staff person." I pointed. "Write those under suspects."

"How'd the person figure out where the statues were hidden?" Sam sighed and rubbed the back of his neck. "I mean, how'd they get to the second one before you did? If they walked up to the library lady and asked for the second clue, the police would've questioned that person instead of us."

I nodded. "Yeah, but they didn't say if they had anyone else to question. Oh, man! That reminds me." I snatched my cell out of my pocket. "I was supposed to call Detective Morris and tell him about the guy I saw." I dropped the cell onto my lap. "I don't have the number."

Maile scooted off the bed and grabbed a card from her nightstand. "Here's his card."

"Great." I punched in the number.

"Detective Yamada."

Why was he answering this phone? "Hello. This is Leilani Akamai. I thought I was calling Detective Morris."

"He's out, so I'm taking his calls."

"Oh." I gulped and wished I didn't have to talk to the grumpy one. "Uhh, you came to my house last night about the missing Menehune."

"Did you remember something?"

"Yeah. There was a guy standing near the computer stations." I described the man. "Could I ask you a question?"

"Go ahead."

"I'm guessing no one else asked the library lady about a second clue, since you questioned me and my friends and also asked if we saw anyone acting strange. Is that true?"

"You and your friends were the only people to find the Menehune yesterday. Whoever took the statue didn't get a second clue."

"Oh! I probably should tell you about the statue at the clinic. It was stolen too."

"What?"

"I was there this morning when I figured out the answer to the second clue. The clinic. But when I looked for the Menehune, I couldn't find it. Then I saw the indentation made by the statue and —"

"I'll check it out. Thanks for the call." He hung up.

I pulled the phone away from my ear and stared at it.

"What's wrong?" Maile scrunched her nose and mouth.

"Detective Yamada is kind of scary."

Sam chuckled. "Last night he was a huge jerk."

Maile waved a hand. "When he was at my house I was so freaked. Thought I was going to throw up right on the living room floor."

Sam snorted, which sent Maile and me into uncontrollable laughter.

Sam shook his head and stared at us.

Once the hysterics passed, I adjusted my position on the bed. "Okay, back to the plan." I cleared my throat. "The detective said no one else found the Menehune at the library."

Maile narrowed her eyes. "So how did the thief find the second one?"

"Hmm." I shrugged. "Don't know. Unless …"

My friends stared.

Maile nudged my side. "Unless what?"

"The culprit is one of the people who wrote the clues."

Umikumakolu
(Thirteen)

"Oh, man! You're right." Maile clamped both arms across her chest.

I rubbed my head. "We need to get to the school and find out the names of the people who helped with the Menehune Hunt."

"Okaaaay." Sam tilted his head to one side. "But maybe we should figure out the third clue and see if that statue is missing too."

"Good idea." I picked up the paper.

Maile nudged me. "Read it."

I took in a big breath.

I'm Menehune Number Three and I love to play.
I've been called a real card and I can make people go bananas.
Be careful, I just might pop out at you.

Maile scowled. "These things just keep getting harder and harder. Can't believe you figured out the last one."

"Yeah, well, I probably wouldn't have if I hadn't been at the clinic." I pressed my lips tight. "At first I thought it was at a school, and since ours isn't open yet, I told Kimo to look around the classrooms at summer school."

Sam ran a hand along his jaw. "If Menehune Number Three likes to play, it could be in a park."

I shook my head. "What about bananas?"

He shrugged. "A picnic? Or banana trees?"

Maile drummed her fingers on the bed. "A grocery store?"

"Naw. I doubt anyone would want to play in there." Sam chuckled. "Especially not Mrs. Wong's store. She'd whack you upside the head if she caught you playing around in her place."

"You're right." I smiled at the movie re-run playing in my head of Mrs. Wong screaming at Kimo one day when he was prancing around the store and knocked over a box of candy bars.

"Hmm." Maile stared at the ceiling. "Where else do people like to play?"

Sam rattled off a list. "The beach, the gym, tennis courts, soccer fields, playground —"

"Hold on!" I waved my hands. "Those are all great ideas, but what if it isn't a place where people play?" A smile overtook my mouth. "What if it's a toy store?"

"Cool!" Sam's head bobbed as if his neck was made out of a slinky. "I get it." He reached for the clue. "Okay, so he's hiding there 'cause he likes to play things like card games —"

"And the part about people go *bananas* could be about the card game, Go Bananas!" Maile beamed.

"So we should go check out Toy Land in town." I snatched the clue and shoved it in my pocket. "And I bet the part about *popping out* at us could mean he's hiding near one of those games that surprises you with shooting stuff in the air, or maybe that hot potato game."

Sam stood and clamped both arms across his chest. "Now our

only problem is to get to town. Only Maile has a bike here."

Maile glanced at her watch. "Kainoa should be back from the beach soon. Maybe after we have some lunch he'll give us a ride to town."

I couldn't wait to see Kainoa and show him my cast-free arm. Soon I'd be riding waves right beside him.

The slamming screen door caught my attention as I slurped a big bite of saimin noodles.

Kainoa strolled in. "Aloha! Mmm. Any da kine still deah fo' me?"

"Sure." Maile pointed at the stove. "You can have the rest."

A droplet of water dripped from his Hawaiian print board shorts. His stringy, wet hair bounced in rhythm with his stride. I pictured him tackling and conquering a huge wave and I couldn't help but smile.

Kainoa looked in the pot, snatched a bowl from the shelf, and poured the rest of the noodles into it. Smiling, he approached the table. And sat next to me.

My heart fluttered and heat flooded my cheeks. I gulped some water and hoped my face hadn't turned bright red.

"Hey, Leilani. No mo' cast?"

I grinned, but forced it to stay small. Didn't want to give out any strong vibes. My friends already suspected I liked Kainoa. No way I wanted to give them more ammunition to bullet at me later. "Yeah. Got it off this morning."

"When you hitting the beach?"

I shrugged. "Maybe in a couple days. My mom wants me to work my arm and build up the muscles first before I start surfing again."

He nodded and swallowed noodles. "Sounds smart to me."

Maile stood and walked her bowl and glass to the sink. "Hey, Kainoa. You willing to give us a ride into town?"

"Sure." He gulped half a glass of water then wiped a hand across his lips. "What are you three up to?"

She grabbed Sam's and my bowls. "Still working on the Menehune Hunt."

"Good. Tyler and I have to go to the library today and pick up the second clue."

I frowned ."Did they put a new statue there?"

"No. I think they just put a picture with a note or something. Tyler's cousin is part of the group who set up the whole thing and he told Tyler they didn't have any more statues."

I frowned. "Isn't the library closed?"

"Yup, but staff are there cleaning up, so they have the picture and the info at the front counter. Anyone who's figured out it's at the library can get the second clue." He finished the last of his saimin. "Let's go, guys. Those Menehunes aren't going to wait forever."

Our foursome paraded outside and into Kainoa's truck. Maile squeezed into the tiny back seat since she was the smallest.

Sam motioned for me to slide into the front next to Kainoa. "Ladies first." He sported a little smirk.

I sneered at him, but climbed into the pickup anyway, and passed Kainoa a slight grin.

"Where exactly do you want to go in town?" Kainoa backed the pickup onto the road and shifted gears.

"Toy Land." I laced my fingers together and prayed he hadn't noticed the shaking.

"That's a cool store. Tyler works there." He turned a corner. "In fact, he's at work right now."

"Oh." I cocked my head. "If the statue is there, how can

Tyler be involved in the hunt?"

Kainoa shook his head. "He isn't. I'm doing the whole clue thing. He's just coming along to be a cheerleader."

"Can't quite picture Tyler with pom-poms."

He chuckled. "Funny."

Couldn't help but smile. I longed to be surfing again with Kainoa supporting me. Yeah, like a cheerleader. I snuck a sideways glance. He'd look ridiculous waving around those two gigantic balls of plastic strips.

"Here you go, troops. Toy Land on your right."

The three of us piled out, waved, and hollered our thanks.

Eyes riveted to the retreating truck, I sighed.

"Come on, Leilani. Leave your crush outside and let's get to our mission."

"Maile, I already told you I don't have a crush on your brother."

"Whatever." She clutched my arm and pulled me inside the store.

Sam lumbered behind. "What do we check out first?"

I glanced around the store, then pointed. "Over there. We'll look at all the games that pop, toss, or throw."

We marched to the aisle and dug through the boxes.

Maile held one up. "Hey, this is a cool game."

Sam peeked over her shoulder. "Yup. But stick to the mission."

"Right." She shelved the box.

After several minutes of searching, I groaned. "Man, I thought we were right."

Sam sunk both hands into his pockets. "Maybe someone stole this Menehune too."

"Could be, but I didn't see a place for it to have been on

these shelves. They're too crowded. I think it's somewhere else."
I scanned the area.

"But what else pops?"

"Hmm. The clue said he might pop out at us." I maneuvered
to the end of the aisle and paced along the rows. One caught my
attention. I motioned for Maile and Sam to follow. "This one."

Maile scrunched her nose. "Little kids' toys?"

"Yup." I trudged down the aisle. "Here." I picked up the
multi-colored toy. "A Jack-In-The-Box pops out at you."

"Cool!" Sam beamed. "Always liked those crazy things.
Scared me every time it popped out at me."

I scanned the shelf and noticed the back corner was clear.
Perfect spot for a menehune.

But it wasn't there.

"Man! Someone took this one too." Sam shook his head,
lines creasing his forehead and between his eyes.

"Maybe. Sure looks like it, but we'll have to check with the
counter person." I turned and marched toward the front.

Maile scampered behind me. "Tyler's working, remember?
Maybe he's the cashier today."

I focused ahead and caught site of the guy. "Oh, good. It's
Tyler."

We continued our trek and approached him. I placed both
hands on the glass top. "Hi, Tyler."

He tipped his chin up and grinned. "Hey, Leilani. You, too,
Maile … Sam. How can I help you?"

I gulped. "We think we've found the third menehune."

Sam leaned an elbow on the counter and eyed Tyler. "And
it's gone. Stolen."

Tyler held out his palms. "Hold on. This is only the second
day of the hunt. You can't look for the third one yet."

I shook my head. "We don't care. We're trying to figure out who's taking all of the statues. Tell us if Menehune Number Three was hiding behind the Jack-In-The-Boxes."

His mouth hung at half-mast. "Wait. I'll be right back." Tyler trucked from behind the counter to the back of the store.

I leaned close to my friends. "I don't think he believes us."

Tyler came out from an aisle and raced toward us. He panted as he spoke. "You're right. It's gone."

A shiver snaked its way up my back. "Okay. So, what we need now is the fourth clue."

He shook his head. "I can't do that. Already explained that you're too early. I'm actually supposed to disqualify you."

I pulled the game paper from my pocket. "Disqualify away, Tyler." I shoved it across the counter at him. "All we care about is getting the fourth clue."

He stared at me for a moment. Finally he shook his head and opened a drawer. He signed and dated the form, then scratched the word *disqualified* across it. "I'll get the fourth clue." He leaned over the drawer and reached inside.

Something moving caught my eye. A necklace slipped from under his t-shirt and dangled from Tyler's neck.

A shark's tooth.

ʻUmikumahā
(Fourteen)

Clutching the fourth clue, I sprinted out of Toy World. Maile and Sam flanked each side.

"Leilani, what's up?" Maile double-timed her steps. "You don't need to move so fast. Is something wrong?"

Sam planted his feet and clamped both arms across his chest. "Yeah. What's up? Show us the clue."

Head hung, I sucked in air. "Did you see it?"

"What?" Sam frowned "You're talkin' crazy."

I leaned against a lamp post, my breathing fast and deep. "Tyler was wearing a shark's tooth around his neck."

Maile placed a finger to her cheek. "Ahhh. I get it. Like the one you saw on the library mystery man?" She latched both hands onto her hips. "Lots of surfer dudes wear those."

"Yeah. But Tyler matches the guy in other ways too. He's about the same height and he has dark hair, long and kind of shaggy."

She shook her head, sun-lit hair flying around her shoulders. "I don't think —"

"I know it's not much, but what if he knows about the locations of all the statues through his cousin?" I lowered my gaze and focused on my hand still clenching the paper Tyler had given me.

Maile rubbed her forehead. "You could be right. But if it turned out to be Tyler, it would kill Kainoa. They've been friends forever." She gulped. "No. It just can't be him. We have to find other suspects."

I drew in a breath and let it escape. "Totally."

Sam cocked his head. "I know Tyler's cousin. His name is Jeremy Chin."

After pushing away from the pole, I took a step toward him. "You do?"

"He's a mechanic. My mom took our car to his shop last week. The stupid engine was making a totally annoying sound. Wasn't a squeal like a belt. More like when my bike chain slips. Kept telling Mom it was probably a rod. 'Course lots of things sound like rod knock. But it turned out to be —"

"Sam!"

He raised his hands in mock surrender. "What?"

I opened my eyes wide and cocked my head.

"Enough with the zombie looks. I get it." Sam set his jaw and gulped a breath. "Anyway, while he was checking the engine, he asked if I knew his cousin, Tyler, since he's kinda close to my age."

"Maybe we can talk to this Jeremy about who all's on the committee." I chewed my lower lip with my teeth. "Where's the shop?"

"That end of town." He waved a hand.

The downcast mood frozen on Maile's face thawed a little. "Yeah. I think we need to talk to Jeremy Chin. Then we can see if any of the members might be involved. Because I know it isn't Tyler who's stealing."

I linked arms with Maile and nudged Sam. "Lead the way."

"No pro-blem-o. But what about the clue?" Sam lumbered down the sidewalk. "We gonna figure it out?"

"We have some time. Remember, Tyler gave us this a day early, so no one else should be looking for number four until the day after tomorrow."

Maile waved her hand. "But if it's someone from the committee, they already could have taken all the Menehunes. And we still don't have any motives for this crazy crime."

I sighed. "Yeah. Wish we could find one of the statues that hasn't been stolen."

Sam motioned for us to turn the corner. "Whoever's stealing them still has to figure out how to get them out of the place without someone seeing. Not easy. For real, 'cause one time I tried to steal some cookies my mom made for her Bible study group." He snatched a quick breath. "You have to create a diversion, like the fire at the library. 'Course, haven't heard of any other fires. Not a clue how they're doin' it." He shrugged. "Maybe they haven't stolen number four yet and we can find it today." He trucked ahead and yelled back. "Or not find it. Ha! Ha! Get it?"

I stifled a giggle and hollered. "We get it, Sam."

Maile grabbed my arm and yanked me down the street. "We'd better keep up or Sam will get to Tyler's cousin, grill him, and solve the case before we take one step inside the shop."

"Okay. But you can let go. I'll get there myself."

"Sorry." She loosened her grip and picked up the pace. "Sam, wait up."

Our threesome trekked down the sidewalk. I spotted a small mechanic shop about a block ahead. Sam stopped in front and motioned, his face contorted as if frustrated because we weren't fast enough.

And, man! Sam could walk fast when he wanted to. Huffing and puffing, I powered through the last few steps. Yeah, I really needed to get back to surfing. My body was suffering from the lack of exercise. I fanned my face, grabbed a water bottle from my backpack, and downed several gulps. After wiping a hand across my wet lips, I eyed my friends and sputtered a few words. "Ready? Let's go in."

Maile and I followed Sam inside. He examined the small shop. "That could be him." He pointed at a guy in coveralls leaning over and reaching under the hood of an old, muddy truck.

The place smelled rank, like a combination of oil, dirty rags and musty old engine parts. "Sam, you should probably talk to him first and then introduce us." I poked his arm.

"No pro-blem-o." He marched across the concrete floor. "Hey."

The guy turned around. "Oh, hey, man." His smile produced cute dimples on either side. "I remember you from the other day. Your mom's car, right?"

He nodded. "I'm Sam. You're Jeremy, Tyler's cousin, right?"

"That's me."

"Didn't mean to interrupt your work, but maybe when you have a break, could you talk with me and my friends?"

He snatched a rag from the ground, wiped off the wrench, and tossed the tool into a nearby chest. "No worries." He opened his arms wide. "This place is mine, so I don't have a boss yelling at me to get back to work." He focused on me and Maile.

"Oh, sorry." Sam wagged an arm toward us. "These are my friends, Leilani and Maile."

He frowned at his greasy palms. "Uhh. Don't think I'll shake your hands."

I grinned. "Yeah. I've had enough gunk and grime for today."

"Me too." Maile's eyes sparkled when she locked her gaze on Jeremy. It had to be the dimples. A guy whose smile coaxed out divots in his cheeks had always charmed her.

Jeremy moved to a shelf, grabbed a clean rag, and wiped his hands again. Didn't seem to do much good. "So what can I do for you kids?" He narrowed his eyes. "Not thinking of becoming mechanics are you?"

Maile beamed. "Nope. We wanted to ask you about the Menehune Hunt. Tyler said you're on the committee."

"Yes, I am." He leaned against the metal shelving. "You trying to find the little guys?"

My heart pumped faster than normal. "We were, but now it seems three of them have been stolen, and we're investigating."

He slapped a hand against his head. "That's right! I knew I recognized you three from somewhere. You're the cute little amateur sleuths who solved the pineapple vandalism mystery."

Cute little amateur sleuths? I gritted my teeth and stifled a scream. "No. Actually we're the *three amazing detectives* who solved it."

His eyebrows peaked like little mountains. "So you're trying to figure out who took the statues? I heard there was one missing after the fire at the library, but I haven't heard about any others."

Sam jumped in. "Leilani figured out the second clue today, and we all worked on the third one. Not supposed to look for number three 'til tomorrow." He shrugged. "But we did anyway, 'cause we're pumped about the real crime, not the game. Tyler told us you were with the planning group. I remembered meeting you when my mom's car went all whacko. Remember that crazy noise?" Sam waved a hand in front of his face. "Doesn't matter.

Anyway, thought you'd have names of the other people who helped."

"Whew! Don't know if I exactly got all that, but if you want the names, I'm happy to assist you in your *detective* work." He made little quotation marks with his fingers when he said the word detective. Then he punctuated it with a snicker.

I squeezed my lips tight. Tyler's cousin irritated me, but I forced my mouth to curve. We needed those names. "Could you also please write down a number for them, too, or maybe where they work?"

He shrugged and grabbed a pad and pencil from the shelf. "Okay." He scribbled for a few moments, then ripped the paper from the pad. "Here. Don't know how this will help, but good luck." He handed the list to Sam.

"Cool!" He turned to leave the shop. "Catch you next time our stupid car makes a weird noise."

Maile and I exchanged glances then shook our heads.

Once we were on the street, Sam unfolded the paper. Maile and I peeked over his shoulders. Sam read the list.

Me, Jeremy Chin
The head librarian, Edith Preston
School secretary, Carla Yamada
Clinic Technician, Dan Stewart
I gasped. Dan-The-Cast-Man?

Umikumalima
(Fifteen)

Maile nudged me. "What's wrong, Leilani?"

"That last name on the list. I'm sure it's the cast guy at the clinic."

"Oh, man! And you were there this morning when the Menehune went missing." She sighed. "Do you think he could have taken it?"

I shuddered. "Hope not. But he could have had time to take it from the front counter while I was waiting in the cast room."

Sam wrinkled his nose. "Without being seen?"

"Maggie, the receptionist, said she'd gone to the back for a few minutes. She thinks that's when it was stolen. Since my mom had seen someone come into the clinic who looked like the guy from the library, I figured it was the same person." I locked my eyes on the ground. "Never even thought about it being someone working at the clinic. Especially not Dan-the-Cast-Man."

Maile chuckled. "Is that what you call him? Pretty funny, Leilani."

I nodded, but wasn't in the mood to be entertaining. Bummed and confused, I lifted my chin and focused on nothing in particular down the sidewalk.

Sam opened his mouth and let words tumble. "Yeah, well, I figure'd it was the stranger too. Kinda weird the guy left right after coming in. Wouldn't he have an appointment or something? What a jerk! He could've just waited if he had a question or something." Sam's mouth scrunched to one side and he shook his head. "Totally lame. The guy would probably call the clinic later and complain. My dad hates that. Says lots of idiots —"

"Thanks, Sam."

He grimaced. "Hey, I was on a roll."

I smiled. "It's okay. You always help us think of every angle. And you're right. He could have just been a rude jerk."

Maile jumped in. "Or maybe he took a business card or an information flyer. Your mom said she was reading and didn't pay too close attention after he first walked in, right?"

"Yeah." I reached for the list and Sam stuck it in my hand. I stared at the names. "It's hard to believe that someone as nice as Dan would be involved in a crime." But anyone could be a criminal, and a great detective had to ignore personal feelings and base everything on fact. "We need to visit the clinic and talk with Maggie." I paused. "And probably Dan too."

"Where is it from here?"

"It's a little ways out of town that direction." A weak wave accompanied my turned-down lips. "Do you two feel like a long walk? Maybe we can take a look at the newest clue on the way."

Sam hooted and raised a hand in the air. "Let's do it! This whole missing Menehune thing is weird. Can't wait to find out why any sane person would steal the dorky things."

"That's why we need to figure out the next clue and see if that statue's missing."

Maile rubbed her forehead. "I think we definitely need to

get to the clinic and question Dan, but maybe that can wait."

"Why?" I locked eyes with her.

"We don't have a motive, right?"

Sam and I nodded.

"We've been talking about trying to get hold of one of the statues to see if we can figure out why they're being taken, so I think that's what we need to do first."

Sam frowned. "Yeah, Leilani. Read the clue and get to wherever the Menehune is hiding before the thief steals it."

I raised my hands in surrender. "Okay. You're right. Timing is everything if we're going to solve this mystery. Let's go for it." I slipped my hand in a pocket and pulled out the rumpled clue.

I smoothed the puckers and read.

I'm Menehune Number Four.
If I'm found hiding here, I'll be swept out the door.
Might get yelled at, although I'm not fresh or cold.
But I won't be canned, so I've been told.

My mouth slanted to one side. "Ideas, anyone?"

Sam scowled. "I think we need to accidentally come across the place like you did at the clinic, 'cause this clue is totally weird."

Maile shook her head. "You say that about every one." Narrowing her eyes, Maile studied the words. "It rhymes."

Eyebrows arched, Sam leaned against a lamp post. "Yeah. Someone worked hard on this one."

"We can figure this thing out." I stood on tiptoes, gazed down the street, and pointed. "There's the park. Why don't we sit over there and try to work on the clue."

"Perfect." Maile plodded down the sidewalk.

As Sam trekked beside her, he dug in his pocket and pulled out a candy bar.

I tagged along behind my friends. The late summer sun blazed on my shoulders. Although I wanted to tan my pale left arm, the afternoon rays proved to be too strong. The park with its huge palms, flowering trees and central fountain would provide a shaded haven.

I took advantage of the few quiet moments to think about the confusing case. Three Menehunes stolen. Why? So far we suspected five people. The four people on the list, and Tyler Chin. Telling Kainoa about Tyler's possible involvement would be disastrous. Kainoa would hate me, and my dreams of surfing alongside him again would die. I clenched my teeth and piloted my body toward the park.

Then there was Dan-the-Cast-Man. He just couldn't be involved. I sighed and reminded myself that everyone was a suspect. The people on the list, Tyler, the guy at the library and the person Mom saw at the clinic. Even though I hated to think a certain one — or two — of them could be guilty, I knew that it might be so.

Maile skipped to the fountain. "Let's sit here. I love listening to the water." She perched on the stone edge surrounding the pool.

Sam and I joined her.

Water bubbling and splashing soothed my confused brain. "Okay. Let's figure this thing out." I smoothed the paper and read the clue out loud.

I'm Menehune Number Four.
If I'm found hiding here, I'll be swept out the door.
Might get yelled at, although I'm not fresh or cold.
But I won't be canned, so I've been told.

"Hmm." Creases forming across her head, Maile shifted her position. "Maybe we should concentrate on the key words."

"Good plan." I pointed at each phrase. "So, we have ... *swept out the door, yelled at, fresh or cold, and canned.*"

Sam chewed on his candy bar. "Swept, huh? Maybe a custodian?"

"Good idea." A puff of air escaped my mouth. "But what would yelling have to do with it?"

Maile sat up as tall as her short body would allow. "How about a school? We have custodians there, and maybe the secretaries might yell at the menehune to get out."

Sam shook his head and swallowed. "Makes sense, but what about the fresh or cold stuff?"

"The boys at school are real jerks sometimes."

"Thanks." Sam burped, then stuck more chocolate, peanuts and caramel into his mouth.

Maile scrunched her nose. "Maybe it's about how they can be fresh toward girls, or other times, cold."

"That works." I sighed. "But how could the little guy get canned unless he worked there?"

Sam wiped a hand across his mouth, smearing chocolate onto his cheeks. "This clue doesn't make any sense."

Maile grinned. "But it's the only one so far that rhymes. I think that's way cool."

A frown crept across my lips. "Yeah, but it doesn't help us at all."

A few moments passed as we stared at the paper. I decided to concentrate on the phrase, *yelled at*. "Let's try to think of places where someone would get yelled at."

"If you're noisy in the library." Sam shook his head. "But we already found Menehune Number One there. Doubt they'd hide another one there."

"How about at home when you make your mom mad?" Maile winced. "Happens to me all the time, but whose house would it be?"

"Usually it's me yelling at Kimo." I shrugged. "Or it could be Kimo yelling to my mom about me." I covered my mouth, but a snort escaped. "The truth is, he's the little annoying nerd that causes all the problems."

"Stop!" Sam waved his hands in front of our faces. "You two are being ditzes. For sure, it can't be in one of our houses — or anyone else's. Think of a public place where someone yells a lot." He grabbed a water bottle from his pack. "There's bingo at the church every Monday night. They do a lot of yelling. But not at each other. So … guess I don't have any idea where that stupid statue is." He gulped some water.

Maile propped an elbow on her knee and rested her chin. "If we come up with a couple places, I bet the rest of the clue will make sense."

Pictures of all the businesses in town floated through my head. I closed my eyes and concentrated. Maile and Sam were quiet. The sounds of the fountain rumbled in my ears while droplets of water sprayed against my back. Not Island Games, or the hardware store, or Suzie's Hair Salon, or the antique store …

My eyes popped open and I jumped to my feet. "I've got it!"

Umikumaono
(Sixteen)

Mouths hanging open, my friends stared at me.

I motioned my arm in a big arch. "The whole clue makes sense now."

"Sit down and tell us what's up, Leilani." Sam punctuated his command with a long belch.

"Gross, Sam!"

He ignored me and downed the rest of his water.

I sat, held the paper close to them, and pointed. "First, the yelling part." I passed a sly grin to Maile and Sam. "Can't believe you two didn't think of this. I know you've both been the victims of yelling at this place." I waited to see a glimmer of realization on their faces. Nothing. "Wong's Market."

"Oh, man!" Maile slapped a hand to her forehead. "Can't believe I didn't think of that."

"I get it." Sam nodded. "Mrs. Wong is always yelling at kids when they touch the fruit. Sometimes she yells even when they don't do anything. She hollered at me once when I was just looking at the mangos. Like she was psychic or something and saw me in the future, reaching out to touch them. Freaked me out big-time when I was a kid. Ever scare you guys? Haven't been back since the whole mango thing."

"She's always after Kimo." I giggled. "The little pest drives her more crazy than he does me."

Maile squinted. "So, if Mrs. Wong is the person who might yell at the Menehune, then I'm guessing the part about not being fresh or cold means he's not hiding in the fresh food or the frozen foods."

I nodded.

"Not with the cans, either." Sam grinned.

"Yup. You two are good." My heart pumped a little faster. The answer fit the clue. "And the last piece about being swept out the door must mean he's hiding in the cleaning products aisle."

Sam jumped up. "Let's go! Gotta find that statue no matter what Mrs. Wong does to us. Hurry, you slugs, before whoever the culprit is can steal it." He grabbed his pack and jogged out of the park.

Maile stood and powered after him. "Sam's gonna get there first and Mrs. Wong will yell at him for sure."

A chuckle gurgled in my throat as I took up the rear. "And then we'll have to deal with the devastation." I couldn't decide if I worried more about Sam or Mrs. Wong.

Before entering the market, I peeked around the corner of the entry to scout out Mrs. Wong. Up front, she punched keys on her ancient cash register and chattered to the customer. I turned and motioned to Maile and Sam. "Let's go in."

We headed straight back to the household supplies and equipment.

I scanned the shelves. Then I remembered. "The brooms. You guys, it must be with them."

"Over there." Sam nodded his head.

Maile trekked to the end of the row and bent down. Sam and I hunkered behind her and peered into the void behind the long, towering handles.

"Look!" Maile's voice exploded much too loud.

Tromping footsteps echoed in my ears. I cringed.

The three of us popped upright and tried to make a quick exit. But the short woman in a flowered dress and white apron appeared at the end of the aisle.

"What you keeds do?" Hands clamped on her hips, Mrs. Wong confronted us. Deep lines etched her tight face. The sneer was highlighted by black hair in a messy bun pinned on top of her head. "You need git out my store."

I nodded. "Sorry. We were looking for some dish soap."

"What you need fo'? You keeds no wash dish." She waved her hands in wild circles. "Git! Git!"

Our threesome zoomed past the agitated Mrs. Wong. We all towered over her. So, why did this tiny woman terrify us so much?

Once outside, I couldn't help but laugh.

Sam clutched both arms across his chest. "Not funny. That crazy lady still scares me."

"Sorry." I stifled the laugh with a hand across my mouth.

"Hey, at least we found the Menehune." Maile beamed. "It's there behind the brooms, and no one has taken it yet."

"Probably because no one can get past Mrs. Wong." I turned and sauntered down the sidewalk.

"Yeah." Maile sighed. "After I found the statue, I couldn't even take a look at it before she confronted us. Don't know how we'll ever get back in the store, let alone have time to inspect the thing."

The scowl on Sam's face softened. "Remember the fire?"

A grimace now draped Maile's face. "What does that have to do with anything?"

"Don't you remember?" Sam sighed and rolled his eyes. "A diversion. That's how the thief got Menehune Number One."

"Duh!" I raised my eyebrows and nodded. "And now we're going to get the fourth one."

Maile stepped backward and waved her hands. "Oh no! I'm not taking any chances with that weird Mrs. Wong. I'd be afraid she might capture us, put us in a dungeon, and cook us up for dinner."

Sam and I laughed until the hysterics made us bend over in pain.

Arms clamped on her hips, Maile stared at us.

Sam sputtered his words. "Can't believe you're as big a wimp as me, Maile."

"I was being funny."

"Yeah, right. Like I believe you."

"Okay, you two." I wagged a finger at them. "I think Sam is right. We do need a diversion. Then we can go into the store and grab the Menehune."

Maile cocked her head. "Grab it? As in steal it?"

"Not really." My eyes narrowed. "Kind of like borrowing it for a while. I mean, just to take a close look at it."

Maile glared at me.

"We wouldn't have time to examine it in the store, so we need to take it."

Sam jumped in. "Leilani's right. We can't have a diversion go on forever, so we'll need to snatch it, then take a look later."

"Okay." Maile raised her hands in surrender. "Just a couple questions. Who's going to steal the thing?"

"I am." Lowering my chin, I spoke to my slippers. "I'm the

one who got you two involved in all this detective stuff, so I'll take the risk."

Maile's voice rose a notch or two. "But that means Sam and I have to be the distraction, and I don't think that's any safer than being the thief."

Lifting my head I riveted my gaze on Maile. "Nope. Not you guys."

"Huh?" Sam cocked his head. "I don't get it. If it's not us, then what? You're not thinking about starting a fire are you? 'Cause I don't want to be arrested for arson. It's bad enough we're going to steal something. Whatcha got that won't land us in jail or in Mrs. Wong's stew?"

A huge smile spread slowly across my face.

"Kimo."

Umikumahiku
(Seventeen)

"Oh, yeah!" Maile nodded. "Your brother could irritate Mrs. Wong to death, or at least drive her crazy."

"Yup. And he's had a ton of practice with her."

Sam slapped a hand against his forehead. "Got it! My main man Kimo wants to be part of The Hawaiian Island Detective Club, right?" He stuck a palm toward us and shook his head, shaggy hair whipping around. "I know! Not the club to us, but to Kimo, it's per-fect-o. I'm up for getting him to help."

"I'll call Kainoa and see if he can pick us up." Maile stepped between me and Sam, linked arms, and pulled us down the street.

Sam groaned and stomped his feet hard with every step, but he didn't yank away from Maile's grip. What a guy he was, to put up with us!

"Maybe my brother will take us to your house, Leilani, so we can pick up Kimo."

"Perfect. I'll give Kimo a call while you talk to Kainoa." I lurched to an abrupt stop and unearthed my cell.

Maile circled us, dancing a little jig. "I'm so excited. Aren't you guys? Why am I the only crazy one jumping around?" A little sneer dressed her lips. "Well, I don't care. I can't wait to solve this case and get our picture in the paper again."

"Shhhhh. I'm trying to call Kimo."

She sighed and pushed buttons on her cell.

Mom answered. "What are you and your friends up to this afternoon?"

"Not much. Just walking around town."

"Do you need a ride home?"

"Maybe, but I'll call. Kainoa might be giving us a ride." My finger found its way to the end of my ponytail and I twisted the hair into a tight coil. "Could I talk to Kimo?"

"Sure." The sound of the phone coming to rest on the table clunked in my ear.

"Hi, Leilani. I've been trying real hard to figure out that clue, but it's a hard one."

"Listen, Kimo." I gulped. My little brother could drive me bonkers, but we really needed him. He'd do a good job. "We need your help."

"For real? Yaaaaaay!"

His yell zapped through the phone and pierced my ear. I winced.

"I'll try hard, Leilani. Where are you? Are you coming home?"

I glanced at Maile who was talking to Kainoa.

"Thanks, Kainoa. See you by the park." She shut her phone and nodded at me.

"Okay, kiddo. Here's the plan. Kainoa is going to pick up me, Maile and Sam. We'll come by the house and get you." I explained the plan to him.

He shrieked. "Cool! I can do that real good, Leilani. Mrs. Wong makes me laugh. She's so funny. See you. Bye."

I giggled and jammed the phone into my backpack. Kimo was the only person I knew who would appreciate Mrs. Wong's nastiness.

"My brother will pick us up over there." Maile pointed and tromped across the street toward the park.

"Wait up!" I raced to catch up with Maile while Sam clomped in big strides behind. "Guess what Kimo said about Mrs. Wong."

Maile frowned. "That she's strange and crazy, and if she catches him she might put him in a dungeon and maybe serve him in a stew?"

I belly- laughed. Sam bellowed and snorted.

"Ha! Ha!" Maile dug fists into her sides and glared at us. "She's one creepy lady."

Clutching my stomach, I managed to spout a few words. "No. Kimo thinks she's funny. I think he loves irritating her."

"For real?" Eyebrows arched above Maile's eyes.

"Yeah, well, that's my weird brother. But I sure am glad he's a little insane, otherwise we'd have to try to distract Mrs. Wong ourselves."

Sam grimaced. "I'm happy my bud's hangin' with us on this one."

"Hey! There's Kainoa." Maile waved at the approaching truck.

He pulled alongside the curb and stuck his head out the window. "Hey, little sistah an' company. Solve any crimes today?"

Maile pulled herself into the tiny back seat of the rundown vehicle. She was the only one who could fit there and still be able to breathe. "No, but we've got suspects."

"Suspects? Hey, I was just messin' with you."

Sam motioned for me to scoot in next to Kainoa, then he climbed in beside me.

"So who are you suspecting of what?" Kainoa pressed the gas pedal and the old thing rattled out of town.

Light glinted off the windshield, flashing in my eyes as we passed under a row of palms. I wanted to tell Kainoa about Tyler, but worried about how he might react.

He sighed. "Okay. So you don't want to tell me about your little sleuthing adventure. That's fine."

"Hey!" Maile leaned forward and flicked the back of his head. "Don't forget how we investigated and solved the pineapple vandalism case. It wasn't an adventure — I mean, it was, but it was a real case with real criminals."

"Okay! You don't have to thump me. I have no doubt the three of you will solve another mystery." He glanced in the rearview mirror. "I'm thinking you're working on the disappearance of the library Menehune?"

I squirmed in my seat. "Yeah. But it's more than just that one statue. Numbers two and three are gone too."

"You jokin' me?"

"Nope." Clutching handfuls of tank-top material, I debated how much to tell him.

"Wow! That's weird." He glanced at me.

My lips curved to one side and my heart raced.

"Hope fo' see you da kine beach."

I swallowed hard. Kainoa hoped to see me at the beach, riding the waves, soon. I prayed the hurricane in my stomach would calm. I sneaked a quick peek at his tanned, muscular arms, then at my wimpy, pale one. I'd never keep up with him even if he did let me surf alongside him. But Kainoa was a great teacher and he'd helped me so much in the past. Maybe he'd teach me some cool surfing moves and techniques again.

"Here we are." He turned and caught me gazing at him.

I forced a grin and lowered my chin. "Thanks for the ride."

"Hey, kids!" My mom trotted down the front stairs and

waved. "Come on in and have a snack. I made some brownies."

"Thanks, Mrs. Akamai." Sam jumped from the truck, Maile right behind.

My heart thumped in my chest and echoed in my ears. I locked eyes with Kainoa. "You want to come in?"

He shrugged. "Naw. I'm good." He motioned toward the house. "Maile said the three of you and Kimo might want a ride back to town?"

"Yeah. Do you have time?"

He nodded. "Pau hana."

Good. Kainoa was done working for the day.

"You better get some brownies before my sister, Sam and your brother devour them all."

Praying I would say it right, I gulped. Kainoa should know that Tyler was a suspect. "I'm good." My hands shook and my stomach churned. "Kainoa, I need to let you know something."

"Yeah? Like you'll never ride the waves again?" He grinned. "Funny."

"I thought so. 'Cause I know that would never happen. You're the best female surfer around. I mean, for your age and all."

"Thanks." What a super comment coming from the greatest surfer I'd known. But he only saw me as his kid sister's friend. My heart dropped like a boulder plunging to the bottom of a Akaka Falls. Would he ever see me as more?

I filled my lungs and decided to tell Kainoa about Tyler. "I wanted to explain about our investigation of the missing Menehunes."

"So you really are trying to figure it out, huh?"

"Yeah. So, can I ask you something?"

"Sure."

"When you came to the library, was Tyler with you, or did

THE HAWAIIAN ISLAND DECTECTIVE CLUB

he meet you there?"

He narrowed his eyes and cocked his head. "He told me he'd be at the library, so he'd meet me there and then go with me wherever I thought the first statue might be hidden. I actually thought it would be at Island Games." He frowned. "Why?"

I laced my fingers together and squeezed hard. "Because Tyler's cousin is on the committee that planned this fundraiser. When the police told me to think about who and what I saw before the fire started, I remembered seeing someone." My mouth fell into a frown. "Anyway, today we talked with Tyler's cousin, Jeremy, the one in the planning group. So, Tyler could have found out from him about where the Menehunes were hidden."

Kainoa shook his head. "No. You're wrong."

"The guy at the library and the person my mom saw at the clinic where the second one disappeared matched Tyler's description." My knuckles ached from squeezing. "I don't want to believe that it's Tyler. I really like him. But he has to be a suspect."

Kainoa slammed the heel of his hand into the steering wheel and groaned. "Tyler nevah do da kine. You fo' real?" His fiery eyes flashed at me.

I cringed. "I'm so sorry, but —"

"You lolo to da max."

Of course Kainoa thought I was crazy.

He pointed a finger in my face. "Nah, 'nuff already! Get out of my truck, Leilani!"

Umikumawalu
(Eighteen)

Horrified, I hung my head, pushed the truck door, and slid from the seat. My hands shook and blood pulsed hard through my chest. When my feet touched the ground, the slight jar vibrated my bones as if they were a toothpick tower. I prayed that my lunch would stay put.

"Wait, Leilani."

I stopped after two steps, but didn't turn toward Kainoa.

He took in air and heaved a heavy sigh. "I've done it again, huh?"

Focusing on my polished toenails, I inched myself around toward him. Lifting my chin, I peeked at his stern face.

"I'm blaming you for something ... well, for something good you're trying to do."

My heart clobbered my ribs in double-time.

"Sorry. You're just investigating. Guess a detective has to look at every suspect like he were the culprit."

A tiny grin worked its way across my mouth. "Yeah, for sure." I pinched my lips tight. "But I'm so sorry if —"

Kainoa shook his head. "Don't apologize." He motioned toward me. "Get back in here, surfer girl. Maile, Sam and Kimo should be coming soon."

My grin spreading into a smile, I stepped toward the truck. Kainoa reached out his hand to me.

Avoiding his rich brown eyes and their piercing sparkle, I grabbed his fingers. He slipped his hand over mine in a powerful grip and yanked me back into the vehicle.

My heart and stomach performed gymnastic feats at Kainoa's touch.

"Hey, Leilani!" Kimo's squeal floated from behind. "I brought you a brownie."

I scooted across the worn seat. No way could I handle taking a bite of any food, let alone a brownie.

Maile and Kimo piled into the back and Sam climbed in next to me.

Kimo shoved the snack between me and Sam, along the side of my face. "Don't you want it? It's real yummy."

"Maybe later." I frowned and pushed his hand away. "You can eat it if you'd like. I'd hate to see it get squashed or something."

"Yum!"

I glanced back and saw him chomp a huge bite.

"Thanks, Leilani." He spoke through dark brown teeth and lips, bits of brownie flying from his mouth.

"Gross, Kimo!" Grimacing, I reached back and shoved his forehead. "Close your mouth when you eat."

He swallowed, wiped an arm across his mouth and nailed me with a sneer. "You sound like Mom."

"Thanks for the ride." I was the last to climb out of the truck onto the sidewalk about two blocks from Wong's Market.

Kainoa's eyes nearly disappeared when a smile spread wide across his face. "No problem. You four have fun looking for the missing Menehunes." He winked.

Praying my ribs would keep my thundering heart imprisoned, I flashed a quick smile his direction and turned. The rattling and chugging of the ancient truck faded as Kainoa drove away.

Kimo bounced up and down like a yo-yo gone wild. "Let's go! I can't wait to see Mrs. Wong. She gets so mad." He stopped jumping and bent over in laughter. "Her face gets so red and she stomps around like this." He imitated her.

I couldn't help but laugh. Maile and Sam joined in too.

"Okay, Kimo." I grabbed a chunk of his t-shirt and pulled him close. "We need to plan this thing really well."

His eyes opened wide and flashed like little sparklers. He twisted his hands together. "I'm super excited!"

Maile leveled her eyes with Kimo. "You know it's really important you do a good job, right?"

He nodded.

"Leilani's going to grab the Menehune."

Kimo cocked his head and twisted his mouth. "How come she's gonna do that? Isn't it stealing?"

Sam planted both hands in his pockets. "No, Kimo. Just taking it to investigate the mystery. You know weird ole Mrs. Wong. She'd never in a b'zillion years let us take the thing out of her store. And no way we'd have time to look at it inside." He shrugged. "So, gotta get it outside. Detectives do that diversion stuff." He pushed a finger into Kimo's chest. "That's your job, my man. Then Leilani will grab the statue and we'll take a look at it later."

Kimo grinned. "Do you have a big ole magnifying glass that you're gonna look through?" He pantomimed, looking us over with his imaginary tool.

"This is serious, Kimo." I blasted him with some mean-mouth. "You can't be part of the Hawaiian Island Detective

Club if you think that everything's a joke."

"I don't." He scowled and stood up straight like a soldier facing his commanding officer. "I'll do good. I promise."

"Okay." I pointed toward the market. "You need to go into the store and get Mrs. Wong's attention so she'll follow you outside."

Kimo nodded so hard it looked like his head would fly off.

"Then you'll start fingering all the fruit in the bins."

He beamed. "She hates that."

"Yup. So, your job is to keep her busy by driving her crazy. Then I can slip inside and grab the Menehune, okay?"

"Uh-huh."

Maile shrugged. "What do you want me and Sam to do?"

"You're going to go with me, just in case Mrs. Wong comes back inside and we need to distract her."

Sam clicked his tongue. "Let's go for it!"

"And be careful so we don't get caught." I linked arms with my two friends, and Maile grabbed Kimo's. We skipped down the sidewalk — except Sam who stomped along, shaking his head — as if we were characters from The Wizard of Oz dancing down the yellow brick road.

Sam groaned. "Sure hope none of the guys from school show up right now."

Kimo giggled and skipped faster.

Once we reached Wong's Market, I motioned. "Let's wait here on the side while Kimo gets Mrs. Wong to come outside." I glanced at him. "You ready, kiddo?"

"Yup!" He raced toward the entry and popped inside. "Hi, Mrs. Wong."

Maile, Sam and I plastered ourselves against the wall and waited.

"What you want?"

"Some fruit."

Kimo's footsteps echoed on the wood porch.

"You no touch!" Her steps sounded.

I peeked around the corner and saw her back. Kimo was weaving around the bins, peering inside, and grabbing at produce.

"You dum-dum keed! I say you no touch fruit."

Kimo bounced around some more, just out of Mrs. Wong's reach.

I glanced behind at Sam and Maile and nodded toward the porch. Filling my lungs, I took off in a cautious jog, my friends behind. We ducked through the open door and hustled to the back corner where the Menehune hid behind the brooms.

Hands shaking, I felt a shiver in my spine. I slipped the backpack from my shoulders, squatted, snatched the statue, and tucked it into my bag. My heart hammered in my ears and something in my stomach churned and crashed like primo surfing waves.

"Good job, Leilani. Now let's get out of here." Maile grabbed my arm and yanked me to a standing position.

Sam followed behind as we wove our way through the aisles.

Mrs. Wong was still doing battle with Kimo outside. She flailed her arms and hollered. "You git! I no like no dum-dum keed come my store, touch fruit. You buy or git."

"Okay, Mrs. Wong." He dug in his pocket. "Ahh! I forgot my money." Kimo put on his best whine and stomped his foot. "I really wanted a mango."

"I call police if you no git."

Our threesome dashed outside and headed for cover.

"Bye, Mrs. Wong." Kimo's footsteps pounded on the wood porch.

Peeking from around the corner, I caught sight of him approaching and Mrs. Wong throwing her hands in the air while looking into the sky. "What I do?" She stomped inside, shaking her head. "Deez dum-dum keed touch fruit. Make me crazy." Her voice faded.

Kimo lurched around the side of the building. "Did you get it? Huh? Did you?"

"Yeah." I grabbed his arm. "Let's go."

We trekked down the sidewalk.

I pressed a hand on my forehead. "I feel ill. And my legs won't move another step."

Maile tugged my arm again while Sam and Kimo pushed from behind.

"You guys! Don't you realize what I just did?" I shuffled along.

Sam plodded up beside me. "Yup. You've saved the day, and now you're gonna solve the missing Menehunes' mystery. You loved solving the whole pineapple thing." He paused and twisted his mouth. "Hmm. All this fruit and pineapple stuff is making me hungry."

"So what, Sam. I don't care about your super inflated appetite." I waved my hand around and tipped my nose to the sky. "I'm a criminal."

Maile tugged on my ponytail. "You can't think of it that way. We're trying to get clues and figure out why these statues are disappearing." She sighed. "Besides, Sam, Kimo and I are in this too. We're just as guilty as you."

"And I did real good. Right, Leilani?" Kimo's eyes grew wide and his smile consumed the rest of his face.

"Yeah, you did." I tweaked his nose, then shrugged. "But I'd sure feel better if this whole robbery thing gives us some answers."

Kimo jumped up and down. "I have an idea." He pointed. "There's Sunset Shave Ice. We could go there, get a snack and look at the little statue."

"You hungry again?"

"Guess so." He shook his head. "I love shave ice. Can we go? Puleeeeeeeze, Leilani?"

"Hey! I thought Mom already promised to take you here this afternoon?"

"Yeah, but then you called, so we didn't go."

Sam's face brightened. "Shave ice sounds good to me."

Of course Sam was ready for food. I sighed. "Okay. We'll sit on the bench." I pointed. "You go inside and get yourself one." I plowed through my pack and found some money. "Here."

"Thanks, Leilani." Kimo pranced into the tiny store.

Sam hollered after him. "Right behind ya."

Maile settled on the bench and motioned to me. "Come on! Let's take a look at the statue. I want to know what's so important about it."

I sunk down next to her and unearthed the Menehune. It was kind of funny looking, but nothing seemed unusual.

Maile grabbed it from my hands. "Looks pretty normal to me." Twisting it over and around, she sighed. "Nothing."

As she rotated it, I noticed the bottom. I reached for the statue. "Let me see it for a second."

Maile handed it over. "Did you notice something?"

"Yeah." I peeled the sticker from the base, revealing a hole underneath.

"Hmm." Maile craned to see. "Could be something inside,

but I didn't hear anything rattle."

I shook it. No sound. I stuck a finger inside and ran it around. Plastic.

"Did you find something?" Maile's eyebrows peaked high.

"Think so." Scrunching my face, I pulled on the thing taped to the inside. It released. "Got it!"

I wrapped the mystery item around my finger and slid it out the hole.

My mouth hung open.

Umikumaiwa
(Nineteen)

Eyes riveted to the tiny plastic bag, I closed my drooping mouth and swallowed hard.

Maile cocked her head. "What is it?" She zoomed in for a closer look. "Looks like …"

I twisted my mouth to one side and nodded. My heart raced and my hands tingled. "Diamonds."

"You sure?" Maile reached for the sack and dangled it in front of her face. "Maybe they're just crystals." She stuck her nose close to the sparkling stones. "But why would anyone hide them inside a dorky statue if they weren't real?"

"They wouldn't." I snatched the bag from Maile. "I'm guessing these really are diamonds and were smuggled here."

Maile sat up straight, her mouth flat-lined. "I get it. Someone's stealing the Menehunes for the diamonds inside." She planted a finger along her temple. "I'm a little confused. How did the statues get into our Menehune Hunt? Wouldn't the smugglers have known where they put the diamonds? And why would they let them get delivered to our school for the fundraiser? This whole thing is totally crazy."

I nodded. "You're right. We have a million questions to answer."

"Thanks for the shave ice, Leilani." Kimo clomped out of the store holding his giant-sized treat like a trophy.

Sam lumbered behind, his face nearly buried in the colored frost.

"What flavors did you get?" Maile jumped up and zipped toward Kimo. "Looks like you got guava. I love that flavor. But my most favorite is mango. Did you get some mango?" She scanned the icy mound.

Sam joined us. "See that part where there isn't any color?" He pointed at Kimo's treat and puffed out his chest. "Coconut, huh? I think maybe that's my favorite flavor. 'Course, not very cool 'cause there's no color." He spooned into the blue part. "Know what the blue is? Could be bubblegum or blueberry."

Kimo wiped a hand across his blue-stained lips and beamed. "You're so cool, Sam. I got guava, coconut and blueberry."

"Mine's bubblegum."

"I like all the flavors. Couldn't make up my mind." Waving his spoon in the air, Kimo trekked to the bench and sat. "You guys figure out anything about the little statues?"

"Yeah." I stuffed the plastic bag into the hole and re-stuck it inside, and the paper plug to the outside. It barely clung to the bottom, but it would have to do. "Now, we need to get this to the police."

"Police?" Kimo spit a spray of ice while speaking with his mouth full.

"Kimo! Yuck!" I wiped pink bits from my shorts. "Swallow before you talk, ding-dong."

He swallowed. "How come you have to go to the police? Mom's gonna be super mad."

"No she won't. I'm not going to say anything to her." I opened my backpack and stuck the Menehune inside. "We'll go deliver it right now."

"Cool!" Kimo jumped up. "Oops!" His shave ice listed to one side like the Leaning Tower of Pisa. He smacked a hand against the tilting ice and pushed it back to center. He belly laughed. "Did you see that? Almost lost the whole thing, but I saved it."

Laughing I stood up. "Let's go." I slipped the straps of my pack over both shoulders. "On to the police station, everyone."

Maile tucked her hair behind her ears and stood. "You really think going to the police is a good idea? What if they arrest us for stealing the statue from Wong's Market?"

A knot twisted and pulled tight in my chest. Maybe Maile was right. And if we were arrested for robbery, Mom would just die. I rubbed my pounding head, just above my eyes.

Sam leaned against the bench back. "My mom will freak if I get arrested. Man, she'll freak if she finds out what we did at Wong's Market. She'd never be able to shop there again." He shook his head. "She'll for sure say she raised a criminal."

"Whoa, Sam!" I couldn't help but giggle. The knot and pain inside bubbled away like a wave onto shore.

"Not funny, Leilani."

"But, Sam, you *are* funny. We'll be fine."

Maile maneuvered between the two of us and glanced back and forth. "I think I know what we need to do."

Usually Sam was the creative one of our threesome, but when Sam was being weird about stuff, Maile always came through. "Bring it on, Maile. How do we clean up this mess?"

She sucked in a big breath. "Go to Wong's Market and put the Menehune back."

"But why can't I help?" Kimo whined as he skipped beside me.

I stopped, clamped a hand on my hip, and clenched my teeth. "Kimo, I already told you. You did a great job with Mrs. Wong today, but she'll call the police if you show up again. Especially if you do anything to irritate her." I sighed. "You need to stay on the side of the store while Maile, Sam and I go inside to put the statue back." I poked his shoulder. "You're a great member of the detective club, but it means not only do you have to do things, sometimes you have to *not* do things."

He twisted his mouth. "Okay. I get it. I want to be the best detective ever, so I'll stay real quiet outside."

"Good for you, Kimo!" Maile raised her hand. "High-five."

They smacked their hands together, then he turned and did the same with Sam.

Kimo faced me, his hand held high. "Your turn, Leilani."

I grinned and slapped his hand. "Let's get going. I want to get rid of this crazy statue."

We plodded down the sidewalk. The smells in town were different than the ones by my house. Less flowery scents, but more yummy aromas of the bakery and restaurants. As we approached the store, I picked up the smell of ripe fruit sitting in the baskets and bins on the porch. Once I saw the Wong's Market sign, my stomach went sour. I gulped and quickened my step. "Let's get inside and return this guy to his hiding place."

Maile picked up the pace. "So Sam and I will keep Mrs. Wong occupied while you put the statue back, right?"

"Yup." I glanced at Sam. "I'm depending on you to keep talking to Mrs. Wong. Ask her a million questions, okay?"

Sam shot us a serious scowl. "Hey. Can't help talking a lot sometimes." He shook his head. "Don't know if I can just spout a bunch of random stuff at any ole time like a trained circus animal. I'm not some nerdy puppet you know."

I shoulder nudged him. "Don't be such a goof. You can do it." We reached the steps and I stopped. "Ready?"

Maile turned and locked her eyes with mine. "Don't forget to be super quiet so Mrs. Wong doesn't see you when we go in."

"Yeah." I nodded. "Otherwise she'll stomp after me to see what I'm doing." Cocking my head, I smiled at Sam. "You ready for the big show?"

He set his jaw in a stern expression and tipped his head back. "Even if the weird lady grabs me and throws me into a cooking pot, I'll keep talking so you can get away, Leilani."

"Get going, you dork." I shoved Sam. "And if you end up in the dungeon or even on the stove, I'll come rescue you."

Maile clamped a hand across her mouth. A laugh still gurgled from her throat. She shuffled toward the store entry and peeked around the corner. Her hand waved us forward.

"Kimo, you stay here, out of sight, okay?"

"Okay."

Once Sam and I reached the door, I spotted Mrs. Wong stacking boxes near the front counter. Her back faced us. My fingers shook as I formed them into an okay sign and flashed it at Maile and Sam. The air inside the store smelled like detergent and old rags. Grimacing, I spotted the mop bucket in a corner. Mrs. Wong was a nut about cleaning the floors. Just when I finally got my annoying cast off, I didn't want to slip on a stupid wet spot and break another bone. I slithered into the market and made my way to the aisles.

Hidden behind the shelves from Mrs. Wong's view, I glanced at my friends. They nodded, entered the store, and marched toward the counter. Their voices echoed in my ears as I made my way to the cleaning supplies and equipment.

"Hey, Mrs. Wong." Sam's voice.

"What you want?" She paused a moment. I imagined her chubby hands digging into her sides. "You in here while ago. I tell you git."

"Yup." Sam's voice sputtered a bit. "Forgot to grab some candy. My friend's birthday is —"

"You git candy, then git out my store."

"What kind does Leilani like, Maile?"

The rack of chocolate bars, and bags of hard and gummy sweets were located on the back wall near where Mrs. Wong was working. *Great plan, Sam.*

"Let's see." Maile's voice. "Not sure. Maybe something chocolate."

"Naw. Don't think she's a chocoholic. Remember her last birthday? She told her mom to make a white cake with whipped cream and mango. Don't think Leilani ever eats chocolate. Maybe she's allergic or something. Oh, man! What if we gave her chocolate and her face swelled up like a beach ball with all kinds of ugly red bumps and stuff?"

I had to stifle a giggle. Sam was doing a great job. Visions of him imitating my puffy face danced through my mind.

The cleaning aisle was in front of me. I turned.

"How 'bout the gummy worms? I love those slimy, gooey things. 'Course if she hates them, well, she'd think we were weird giving her such a gross gift." He bellowed.

The sound of a crinkling package touched my ears.

"I know!" Maile again. "We can give her a bag of the little red hot candies."

Once I reached the cleaning tools, I squatted, dug in my backpack, and replaced the Menehune. My hands shook as I set the statue behind the tall brooms. Now to make my way to the front and out of the market.

"I kinda like those hot things, too, but not as much as —"

"You pick now!" Mrs. Wong's voice overpowered Sam's.

My eyes glanced upward as I prayed Sam wouldn't freak.

"You don't know Leilani, huh? Nope. 'Cause if you did, you wouldn't push me into hurrying. She's a total picky-roonie. If I don't get this right she'll hate me forever, or maybe even sock me in the stom —"

"Out my store!"

I peeked around the corner of the front aisle and located my friends. Maile wrung her hands, her expression tight with lines. She glanced toward me and I flashed a round sign with my fingers. Relief draped her face. She nodded.

The exit in sight, I darted through the open door.

But not before Mrs. Wong's voice and her pounding steps reached my ears.

"Hey! Why you run? What you do my store?"

Iwakalua
(Twenty)

"Come back, you dum-dum keed."

I picked up the pace as Sam's voice faded in the background. "Hey, Mrs. Wong! I gotta pay for ..."

Thank goodness for Sam's gift of babbling.

Kimo jumped out from the corner and I plowed into him. He fell backward onto his behind. "Ouch! Man, Leilani, what happened?"

"We have to hide and wait for Maile and Sam." I grabbed his arm, pulled him up, and dragged him around the corner to safety. Finger to my lips, I flashed him a you'd-better-be-quiet look.

Sounds of car engines, people talking, and birds chirping reached my ear, but there was no crazy ranting from Mrs. Wong.

Footsteps thundered across the porch and down the steps.

"Leilani? Kimo? You guys there?" Sam's voice.

Kimo in tow, I edged around the corner. "Mrs. Wong isn't after you, is she?"

Sam chuckled. "Nope. Guess she figured getting money from me was more important than snatching you."

"Ha! Very funny. I almost believe you. She'd do it, and cook me up in a stew too." I glanced at my shaking hands. "Sure am glad that's over. I was afraid Mrs. Wong would hear my knees knocking together or maybe my heart thundering."

Sam shoved a bag in my face. "Here ya go. Told Mrs. Wong I was buying them for you, so they're all yours."

"Thanks." I grabbed the paper sack. "What did you end up getting?"

A glint in Maile's eyes flashed my direction. "It's a surprise."

Her excitement worried me. I peeked inside, then burst into laughter.

Dum Dums.

After jogging halfway through town to escape any possible chase by Mrs. Wong, we hunkered down on a curb and sucked on Dum Dums.

Maile swung her dum dum pop in the air. "We need to plan our next move."

"Yup." I dug in my backpack and pulled out a notebook, pencil and the list we got from Jeremy Chin. "I think we need to eliminate some of the suspects."

Sam twisted his mouth to one side. "And how we gonna do that?"

"I know!" Kimo jumped up and danced around us, his candy wagging in the breeze like palm fronds.

"Kimo, sit down." I grabbed the corner of his t-shirt as he zipped past. "If you have ideas, you can share them, but tomorrow, Maile, Sam and I are going to do this on our own."

"Ah, man! I wanted to help." He plopped onto the curb and stuck the pop in his mouth.

Maile nudged Kimo. "You helped us a whole lot today. We were all afraid to face Mrs. Wong, but you did it, and helped us find the fourth Menehune."

Sam jumped in. "Yeah, buddy. And if you got ideas now, spill 'em."

Kimo rubbed a hand across his sticky mouth. "Okay. I have one."

Ready to write, I placed the pencil tip on my notebook. "Whatcha got?"

A grin stretched across his lips. "Just ask them."

"Huh?" I frowned. "That won't help. The real criminal will lie."

"Wait a minute." Maile rested a finger on her cheek. "Kimo might have something. If we ask each person on the list where they were during the time the Menehunes were taken, we could eliminate anyone who has a rock-solid alibi." She beamed. "I feel so much like a real detective."

"Hey, we are real detectives." I scribbled *alibis* in my notebook. "Good idea Kimo and Maile." I delivered a sideways glance at my brother and smiled.

He stretched up tall and poked his chin up high. "I'm a great detective."

I waved my pencil in the air. "Okay, so I think it's kinda late today, but tomorrow we can talk with each person on the committee."

"And Tyler?" Sam cocked his head.

"Yup." Tingles scampered up my arms. I reminded myself to keep personal feelings out of my investigating. Tyler was a great guy, and a good friend to Kainoa, but he had access to the first Menehune at the library, and the third one at the toy store. And of course, he also matched the description of someone Mom saw at the clinic where the second statue disappeared.

"So, who first? I'm thinking the technician guy. You said he was pretty cool, right, Leilani?" Sam snatched some air, but it wasn't a long enough pause to let me answer. "I know you don't think he has anything to do with stealing the statues, but we need to ask the guy. He had opportunity at the clinic. Should ask him about the others too. Could have been at the library or the toy store."

"You're right, Sam. The clinic is a good place to start. Then we can go to the library and the school." I chomped on the end of my pencil.

"Then to Tyler's." Elbows resting on her knees, Maile sunk her chin into her palms. "Kainoa's gonna hate that we're investigating his best friend."

"He already knows."

"What?"

"I told him when we were waiting for you, Sam and Kimo at the house."

Maile grimaced. "Did he go ballistic?"

"Yeah, at first. He even kicked me out of the pickup."

"Oh, man! I can understand he'd be upset, but he knows what we're doing and how important it is to look at every possible suspect."

"It's okay. He figured it out by himself." I shrugged and focused on my lap. "He apologized and helped me back into the truck."

"Oooooo!" Using his best sing-song voice, Kimo leapt to his feet and waved his hands around. "Leilani's in love!"

"I am not in love." I tugged on his shorts until he dropped onto the curb. "And if you keep saying stuff like that, I won't let you help us anymore."

Kimo scowled for a moment. Then he zipped his fingers across his lips and nodded.

"Good." I turned toward my friends.

They both snickered.

I grimaced and flung a growl their direction. "What time do you want to meet at the clinic?"

Sam raised and lowered his shoulders. "Ten o'clock works for me."

"What about you, Maile?"

"I'll be there. Kind of excited to meet this Dan guy." Maile opened her bright green cell phone. "I'll call Kainoa and see if he can pick us up."

"More Dum Dums?" I held some up and everyone grabbed one.

"Okay. Kainoa's on his way." Maile closed her phone and pocketed it. "We're supposed to meet him by the park."

Our foursome trekked down the sidewalk. We told stories, mostly about our scary experiences with Mrs. Wong. Laughter wrapped around us all the way to the park. We barely settled in by the fountain when the familiar chugging sounds hit my ears.

Kainoa's old contraption pulled to the curb. I opened the passenger door and stared up at his face, hoping to see a friendly flicker in his eyes.

He smiled and offered his hand in assistance.

Relief flooded over me. I hadn't just imagined his apology earlier, and he hadn't, during the past few hours, changed his mind. Hand in his, I hoisted up and onto the seat. "Thanks."

Kimo climbed into the truck like a wiry monkey and scooted into the back with Maile. Sam hunkered down next to me.

"I'll head to your house first, Leilani." Kainoa flicked the blinker and eased onto the street. "You sleuths find your criminal today?"

Sam grunted. "Only if you count Mrs. Wong."

"Huh?"

"Nothing. She's just kinda weird scary."

Kainoa nodded. "I know what you mean. She hated me when I was a kid. But I always thought she was kind of funny."

"Hey, me too!" Kimo leaned into the front from the back seat and raised a hand toward Kainoa. "High-five!"

"High-five, my man." He smacked Kimo's palm.

"These guys are so afraid of her, but she's just a silly lady. Makes me laugh."

"Just wait until she serves you for dinner." Sam reached a hand out and thumped Kimo's forehead.

"Ouch! She wouldn't do that." Kimo grinned. "She likes me."

His comment started an avalanche of laughter.

About the time the howling calmed, we pulled into our drive.

Kimo opened the door and jumped from the truck.

I glanced at Kainoa. His smile slanted to one side. Barely able to hold his gaze, I stumbled over my words. "Um, thanks for the ride." After Sam jumped out, I slid to the edge and lowered myself to the ground.

Once Sam resettled in the truck, my friends waved as they pulled away.

Including Kainoa.

The big comfy chair in my room awaited me, but I chose to flop onto my bed instead. Another amazing day of investigating. It seemed we'd discovered so much, but then it created so many more questions. I took hold of my pack and dug inside. Several items were extremely necessary. My notebook, pencil and a Dum Dum. I stuck the candy in my mouth and scribbled some notes.

Things to Do in the Menehune Mystery:
1. *Interrogate the five suspects.*
2. *Eliminate those with solid alibis.*
3. *Add suspects to the list if they come up during the interrogations.*
4. *Make a list of how the statues with diamonds might have gotten into the school fundraiser game.*
5. *Figure out if we needed to do a stakeout somewhere.*
6. *Come up with possible culprits and scenarios — motives.*

Scanning the list, I beamed. We were going to catch a criminal and solve our second mystery of the summer.

Then I'd go surfing.

My head cradled in a soft pillow, I stared at the ceiling and imagined trudging through the sand, surfboard under my arm. Sprays of grit flew behind me with every step. The late summer sun shined bright and hot. A slight breeze rustled the palm frond canopies along the edge between road and sand. Kainoa stood along the shoreline, the backdrop of waves breaking in rhythm. Each crash sent a bolt of excitement through my body. After a summer void of surfing, I was going to take the plunge. Drawing in a huge breath of salty air, I picked up the pace. Kainoa held his hand high and motioned for me to come with him. After I reached the water —

The tune blaring from my cell jolted me out of my daydream. I answered without of looking at the caller's number.

"Hey, Leilani. It's Tyler Chin. I hear you think I'm a criminal."

Iwakaluakumakahi
(Twenty-One)

The phone shook against my ear. I prayed the uncontrollable nerves in my hands would calm. "Tyler, I —"

"It's okay, Leilani. I didn't mean to upset you." He paused. "Well, maybe a little. But mostly, I just wanted to let you know that it wasn't me who took any of those Menehunes."

"Tyler, I'm sorry." I sat upright. "But we have a list of suspects, and even though I believe you, we have to investigate everyone who had opportunity."

The sound of Tyler releasing a breath wafted through the phone. "Kainoa was right. You do sound like a real detective."

Jaw held tight, I squirmed. Just because I wasn't some middle-aged, lonely man with a gun, trench coat and hat, I still was a real detective. "Listen, my friends and I were planning on visiting you tomorrow to ask you questions. If you have time, I could ask you right now."

Silence.

"Tyler?"

"Yeah … yeah, why not? Ask away. I'm totally innocent."

"Okay." I grabbed my notebook and flipped to a blank page. "First, were you at the library yesterday?"

"Yeah. You saw me there. With Kainoa, remember?"

"Of course I do, but I mean were you there before I saw you? Were you inside the building?"

No words. Then a huff. "Yes, but that doesn't mean I pinched the statue."

"It's okay. Don't worry about anything but telling the truth. If you didn't take the Menehune, it will all work out. I promise I'll find the person who's been stealing them."

"Great." Tyler groaned. "What else do you want to know?"

A lump formed in my throat. Worried the words wouldn't come out, I swallowed hard. "Were you at the medical clinic earlier today? The small one in town where —"

"I wasn't at any medical clinic today, big or small. Why would you ask me that anyway?"

Irritation brewed inside. "Tyler, I need to ask these questions. Please just answer them, okay? I'm trying to make sure you can be eliminated as a suspect."

He grunted, frustration seeping through the phone. I could picture his scowling face. "Okay, I'll be good and answer your stupid questions."

Clenching my teeth, I willed myself not to stomp my feet and scream. Why was Tyler acting like this? I shuddered at the thought maybe he was hiding something. A deep breath calmed my storming insides. "What time did you go to work today?"

"I don't see what that matters to —" A loud sigh came through the phone. "Sorry. I started work at noon."

The messy scribbles in my notebook were hard to read. But I continued to make notes. If Tyler didn't go to work until noon, he could have been at the clinic in the morning. He was also in the library before the statue was taken and the fire started. Tyler had opportunity to take numbers one and two, and since he worked at Toy World, he could have stolen number three too. But did he know about the diamonds? I made more notes. Tomorrow I'd talk with Maile and Sam about the whole smuggling motive.

"Thanks, Tyler."

"Yeah, well, I hope you don't think I could ever steal anything, let alone those dumb statues."

"I really do believe you, but it's important that I talk with everyone who could be involved."

"What made you think it was me, anyway? I mean, yeah, I was at the library and I was working at Toy World, but what makes you think I'm a primo suspect?"

A shiver wormed its way up my back and across my shoulders. I shouldn't say too much to Tyler. I didn't want him to panic about the whole matching description, sharks tooth necklace and opportunity. "You had opportunity when at the library yesterday, that's all. Thanks for answering my questions. I'll let you know if anything else comes up."

"Anything else?"

I rushed a goodbye to end the conversation as soon as possible. Clicking off my cell, I allowed a long moan to escape my mouth. Then fell backward onto my bed. I did *not* want to do that again anytime soon.

My phone played a little tune and I cringed. Was Tyler calling back?

A quick glance at the screen told me it was Maile.

Before I could say anything, her voice squealed through the phone. "Leilani, turn on the TV. Now!"

She told me which station and then clicked off in my ear. My mouth hung open, but I never got in a word. Maile doesn't usually act crazy. She was seriously upset about something.

I dashed to the living room where Kimo was hunkered down, watching some Disney movie. "Where's the remote?"

He gawked at me as I stormed toward him, hand outstretched. "Hurry! Give it here."

"How come? I'm watching a movie. You can't change the channel."

I spotted the control tucked partway under a pillow next to Kimo. Snatching it, I frowned his direction. "This is important. Your movie can wait two seconds." My fingers shook as I punched in the numbers. What could be so important on TV? Sure hoped Maile wasn't being overdramatic about some hunky guy in a romance movie. The screen blinked and a commercial appeared. If Maile was being silly, I would sic Kimo on her.

"A stupid commercial?" He jumped to his feet. "Mahhhhhm!"

"Just wait. Maile says it's important. And if it isn't, well, I'll let you have at her."

Kimo burrowed into the couch and slammed his head into the back. "Man!"

Mom's footsteps paraded down the hall. "What's wrong now, Kimo?"

After a quick glance at his scrunched face, I hollered. "It's okay, Mom."

Her footsteps retreated as the voice from the TV caught my attention.

"Coming up next, the strange story of missing Menehune statues."

Iwakaluakumalua
(Twenty-Two)

Kimo leaned forward, eyes glued to the screen. "Wow! The Menehune thing is going to be on the news."

Stunned, I sank into the sofa.

Once a short commercial ended, the reporter's face appeared on screen. "And now, an exclusive seen only on this station. It has come to our attention that a strange burglary case is happening in our small town." The man went on to explain the details of the school fundraiser. "This afternoon, a fourth statue was found missing at Wong's Market."

A breath caught in my throat.

Kimo stared at me. "I thought you put that one back, Leilani."

"Shhhhh!" I flashed blazing eyes his direction. "I did. You need to be careful what you say. No one's supposed to know anything about our investigation, especially what happened today."

The voice on the TV continued. "Earlier, we interviewed the owner of Wong's Market."

Bouncing on the sofa, Kimo screeched. "Way cool! Mrs. Wong's gonna be on the news."

Waving a hand at my annoying little brother, I focused on

the screen.

"Mrs. Wong. Tell us what happened."

The familiar piercing voice answered. "I go back my store. Menehune gone!"

"Any idea who could have stolen the statue?"

"Two girl, two boy. Day come my store, drive me crazy, touch evyting. I say git, but day no git. Dose dum-dum keed, day take Menehune."

"Police are now looking into the case, but say they have no motive as to why anyone would be stealing the statues. We will keep you updated as more information surfaces in this strange case of Menehunes Missing."

My stomach squeezed tight and little bumps formed on my skin. Clamping both arms across my chest I rubbed them in an attempt to send the tiny swells away.

Kimo burst into a belly laugh. "Mrs. Wong is so funny! She's more fun to watch than my movie." He snatched the remote from my hand. "But she's gone now, so I get to go back to my station."

"Thanks, kiddo." I dragged myself down the hall and into my room. Shuddering at the thought of police visiting my house again, I collapsed onto my bed. Visions of the reporter, Mrs. Wong, the police and our suspects danced through my head. Exhausted, I decided the best thing to do was get some sleep and deal with suspects tomorrow.

I grabbed my phone to text Maile and Sam. Before I could push a button, the cell beeped. Two texts came in at once.

The first from Sam. *crazy weird*

The second from Maile. *im scared*

I returned both. *no worries. i have a plan.*

Breakfast the next morning was cereal. Kimo hadn't gotten up yet. I figured that he'd stayed up way late watching movies and was sleeping in. I smiled at the thought of him so excited about being done with summer school.

Then I realized I'd forgotten all about the conference yesterday morning. "Hey, Mom, how'd Kimo do in his math class?"

"Good." She finished pouring her coffee and joined me at the table. "His teacher was happy about his progress and I'm very proud of him." She chuckled. "I think he's learned a lesson. Bet he'll be trying a lot harder in school this year. He doesn't ever want to go to summer school again."

I shook my head. "Yeah, well we were both trapped this summer. Me in a cast and Kimo with math."

"I need to go shopping this morning. You want a ride anywhere?"

"Yeah. The library."

"That's right, they're open again. Heard it on the news last night."

Glad that was the only story she'd picked up off the news. The whole Wong's Market thing would have made her freak. "Kainoa said it would take only a day or so to clean up the mess at the library."

"You're not still hunting for those statues, are you? I thought the whole game's been cancelled."

I shrugged. "Yup. But thought I'd check on things there."

Mom scowled. "You and your friends aren't thinking of trying to figure out who's been taking the Menehunes, are you? 'Cause I know you figured out the whole disaster with the pineapple fields, but I don't want you getting involved in anything dangerous."

"We won't." I meant it, but I also knew I wouldn't back down from danger. No use saying anything to worry her. She still didn't know all the details of the plantation mystery, and I was determined to keep it that way.

Mom glanced at her watch. "Be ready in five minutes. I'll leave a note for Kimo." She shook her head. "I may have to threaten him with summer school next year if he dares to get into any trouble."

I grinned. "I'm sure he's looking forward to dropping himself in front of the TV to watch movies and play video games all day."

"Yeah, well, I'm not planning on being gone long. Maybe he'll still be in bed when I return."

I ran to my room and texted my friends: *meet me at lib in 10*

By the time I loaded into the car with Mom, both Maile and Sam had returned my message. I was sure they were anxious to hear my amazing plan. Hmm. Better come up with one soon.

Air blew through the open car windows. Even though I couldn't see the beach or the ocean, the salty scent tickled my nose. I settled backward into the headrest and closed my eyes. Breathing in an extra large amount of the tropical smells, I worked on ideas.

This, of course, didn't last long, as my mind shifted to scenes of breaking Hawaiian waves and surfers bobbing in the water, waiting for the perfect ride.

Sunlight spilled into the big SUV and stroked my face and arms. It heated my left arm with gentle warmth, unlike the sweaty, suffocating sensation when imprisoned in the plaster cast. I smiled and pictured myself riding one of those perfect waves.

"Here you go, sweetie."

I hated to open my eyes and face the day, not to mention Maile and Sam. "Thanks." I frowned and pushed the door open.

"You okay?"

I shot Mom a quick smile. "Yeah. Just hated to leave my daydream."

"Bet it involved surfing, huh?" She leaned to one side and peered around me. "Isn't that Maile and Sam on the steps?"

I nodded, shut the door, and turned. As I jogged toward my friends, I picked up Mom's voice yelling. "Call if you need a ride later."

I waved a hand and continued my jaunt toward the stairs.

Sam jumped up, donut in hand, sporting a powdered sugar mustache. "Leilani! Hey, Ms. Super-Detective, hope you got a plan. Biggo mess — Mrs. Wong on TV spouting off about us. I totally freaked. I thought that she might describe us or something." He smacked a hand to his chest and burped. "And I told you my mom would go ballistic if she ever found out what went down at the market yester —"

"Okay, Sam, I get it." I plopped onto a stair next to Maile. "Believe it or not, I'm terrified." A glance at Maile's face told me she was pretty worried too. "But as long as the police haven't come to arrest us, we'll move forward with our investigation."

Staring into her lap at her folded hands, Maile nodded. "Guess you're right." She raised her head and leveled her eyes with mine. "So, are we going to question the library lady?"

"Yup." I stood. "And then …" I slipped the backpack from my shoulders and dug out the list written by Jeremy Chin. "The school secretary, Carla Yamada, and Dan Stewart from the clinic."

Sam stood. "What's that library lady's name?"

I glanced up from the list. "Edith Preston."

He chomped on the donut. "Think she's the same one?" Bits of the white powder flew from his mouth as he talked.

The little scowl I sent Sam's direction met with a return sneer.

Maile pushed herself up. "If she isn't the one we talked to before the fire started, it should clear her, right?"

"Possibly. But we still need to find out if this Edith Preston was here when the fire started, whether or not she's the librarian we talked to when we found the Menehune."

Sam nodded. "Let's do it." He swung his arm up high and thrust it forward as if to lead us into battle, then marched up the steps.

I grabbed Maile's arm and we trucked behind him.

As soon as we entered the building I noticed the librarian at the counter — same heavy-set, gray-haired lady who'd helped us the other day. I approached and rested my forearms on the shiny surface. "We're looking for Edith Preston."

"I'm Edith. How can I help you youngsters?"

"My name is Leilani, and these are my friends, Maile and Sam. Maybe you remember us from the other day when we found the first Menehune under the computers?"

"Oh, yes!" She scowled. "So sorry about the fundraiser being cancelled."

I nodded. "Thanks. Do you mind if we asked you a few questions?"

"Wait a minute." She wagged a finger at us. "Aren't you the three kids who solved the vandalism case at Tong Plantation?"

Passing her a shy smile, I nodded.

"Well, then, ask away. I always fancied myself an amateur detective when I was a kid." She tucked a strand of the frizzy silver hair into the bun perched on top of her head. "Pretty exciting to hear about kids who actually did solve a mystery."

I glanced at Maile and Sam. Maile sported a huge smile and sparkling eyes. Sam finished up the last of his donut and wiped his hand on his t-shirt. I couldn't help but smile at the librarian's comments, but quickly re-focused on the mission. "Mrs. Preston, did you notice anything strange that day?"

"Strange?"

"Yeah. Like maybe someone hanging around that seemed out of place?"

"Hmm." Lines creased her forehead. "The police asked me the same question. I told them there was one young man hovering around the computer area." Her eyebrows peaked. "Do you think he had something to do with stealing the statue?" She slapped both hands to her cheeks. "Oh my! Or maybe even the fire?"

I shook my head and reached into my pack for the notebook and pencil. "We don't know. Do you remember what he was wearing?"

"Goodness. Let me think. I don't remember much except the baseball cap. Blue one, I think."

While I jotted some notes, Sam jumped into the conversation. "Ever see him at the back of the library? Or maybe head that direction?"

She frowned. "No. I was pretty much tied to the counter that day." She raised a hand. "But Suzie McConnell's here today, and she was here the day of the fire as well. Maybe she can help you."

I leveled my eyes with the librarian's. "Mrs. Preston, since you were part of the committee that planned the fundraiser, did you tell Suzie, or anyone else about the locations of the Menehunes?"

"Absolutely not! And no one could have obtained the information from me either. I've kept the list at home hidden away. No one but myself has had access to it."

I nodded. "Good." I pressed the end of the pencil against my cheek.

"Let me get Suzie for you." Edith Preston shuffled down the counter and waved toward some book cases. "Suzie, could you come here a moment?"

A young woman with bright red hair and lots of freckles appeared from between shelving. She clutched a book to her chest. Mrs. Preston motioned her toward us. "These kids would like to know if you saw anyone hanging around the back of the library the day of the fire."

"Yeah." She squeezed the book tighter, her knuckles turning white. "I already told the police about it. There was this one guy who was kind of tall with reddish-blonde hair." She hung her head. "I noticed him 'cause I have red hair too. And, well, he was kinda cute."

I scribbled the name *Suzie McConnell* in my notebook. "Was he wearing anything like a baseball cap?"

Suzie pinched her lips. "No. But I did think it was kind of funny ..." She unclenched the book with one hand and motioned down her body. "He was wearing some kind of white jacket that went down to his knees."

I swallowed hard. "Like a medical lab coat?"

Her eyes grew wide. "Yeah, that's what it was."

The description matched Dan-The-Cast-Man perfectly.

Iwakaluakumakolu
(Twenty-Three)

I thanked Suzie, turned, and headed toward the door. I didn't want to lose my breakfast right in the middle of the library.

My friends ran after me as I exited and started down the stairs. Maile yelled. "Hey, Leilani, wait up!"

I slowed, dropped onto a step, and slumped forward, head in my hands.

Sam nudged me with his knee. "You all right?"

A groan simmered in my throat. "I guess. It's just ..."

Maile joined me on the step. "You think the guy in the library was Dan from the clinic, huh?"

"Yup." I glanced at her. "It seems the two most obvious suspects are people I like. Tyler and Dan."

Sam tugged on my arm. "Get tough, Leilani. We need to get on this investigation. The answer won't just jump up and smack us in the face." He dug in his pocket and pulled out a bag of peanuts. "Figure both dudes can't be guilty." He popped some nuts in his mouth. "'Course they could be in cahoots. Think Dan knows Tyler?"

I was too drained to interrupt Sam's chattering. After he took a pause in his ramblings, I stood. "I doubt the two of them are in this together. But you are right about one thing, Sam.

We need to talk with the school secretary, and then head to the clinic."

"Great!" Maile bounded down the stairs ahead of Sam and me.

"About Edith Preston." Sam wiped salt from his face with the back of his hand. "Think she could be a diamond smuggler?" He howled. "Can't you picture her skulking around the shipyards dressed totally in black?"

As I trucked along, the picture forming in my mind was pretty comical. "Funny, Sam. Mrs. Preston was at the front counter the entire time. I doubt she could have started the fire or have taken the Menehune."

"Suzie? She was in the back where the fire started."

I shook my head. "No. Mrs. Preston made a point of telling us how sure she was no one had access to the list. And I tend to believe her. But …"

"What?"

"Neither one of them has a solid alibi. And like you said about Tyler and Dan, there could be two people involved. It's possible Edith Preston and Suzie were in it together."

"Hmm." Sam twisted his mouth to one side and squinted as if deep in thought over the whole mystery.

Smiling, I shoved him forward. "Let's catch up with Maile. She's about halfway to the school already."

We jogged a couple blocks, caught up with our friend, and joined her mad pace.

Maile passed us a sly grin. "You guys figure out the solution yet?"

"Duh!" Sam started babbling, filling our ears with a billion words. Between explanations, theories, chuckling, and crunching nuts, he kept going until we entered the school.

Shoving her hand in Sam's face, Maile narrowed her eyes. "Sorry I asked."

Sam shot her a piercing glare. "Whatever."

The secretary sat at a huge desk loaded with papers, file folders and a small computer. A nameplate balancing partly off the edge said *Carla Yamada*.

We walked forward, and I planted my arms on the counter.

The short, thin woman stood and approached, her long black hair flung back and forth with each step. "Hello, kids. I remember you three from the Menehune Hunt." She tucked one side of her hair behind an ear. "Sorry about everything happening with the statues being stolen."

"Yeah. It's kind of a bummer. And that's why we're here. You were part of the planning team, right?"

She nodded, her eyebrows pulling together.

"On the first day of the hunt, I know you were here, but were you here the entire time?"

She cocked her head. "Sounds like you're trying to investigate. My husband is a police officer and he —"

"Oh! I think I met him the other night." I motioned to my friends. "We all met him. Detective Yamada, right?"

"Yes. Were you at the library when the fire started? I know he questioned a lot of people that day."

I nodded. "Mrs. Yamada, do you mind answering a few questions?"

"Oh, my! I get it now. You're the three who played detective and helped with the vandalism case at Tong Plantation."

We did not *play* detective. It was for real. Sighing, I riveted my eyes with hers and nodded.

"Sure. I'll answer your questions. I think it would be funny if you three solved the case before my husband did." Carla

Yamada chuckled. "He's so serious about his work. Thinks he's the best in the world. Now don't get me wrong, he's amazing, but sometimes I think he needs to relax."

Carla Yamada was totally right. How could such a sweet, energetic person like her be married to such a stone-faced, grumpy man?

"Anyway, to answer your question, I was here the entire day. The head secretary can confirm it." She turned and grabbed a notepad. "Here's her number. She's off work today to get some dental work done, but you can call her." Carla shoved the note toward me.

"Thanks." I tucked it into my pack. "One more thing. Could anyone have gotten the information on the Menehunes from you?"

She shook her head and frowned. "Oh, no. I have the list in my locked drawer here at work. No one else has the key and if someone had broken in and looked at the list, the lock would have jammed. But the lock and list are in perfect shape."

After thanking Mrs. Yamada, we marched outside and began the long walk to the clinic. This gave us plenty of time to talk about the suspects. We all agreed that it was unlikely Edith Preston or Carla Yamada were involved in the crimes. Or anyone they knew. But a good detective keeps an open mind.

Maile halted and leaned forward. "I don't think I can go any further. Is it okay if I call Kainoa and see if he can give us a ride the rest of the way to the clinic?"

I shrugged. "Sure." Every time I saw Kainoa my heart seemed to go into spasms. Then there were my hands. I hated how sweaty my hands became when Kainoa was near.

"Okay." Maile clicked her phone closed. "He'll be here in a couple minutes. Can we sit down now?"

No curbs where we were walking, but there were lots of tall palms. We found a cluster and settled in underneath.

Maile groaned as she adjusted her position. "Man, I'm going to be glad when we get done with all this questioning today."

"For sure." Sam sat, leaned against a palm trunk, and rested both arms on his bent knees. "After Dan, anyone else we gonna see? I'm starving."

Of course Sam was hungry. He'd eaten only enough for a lion to survive, not an elephant. I squirmed, sinking my behind deeper into the sandy soil. "Yeah, I think we missed lunch, but maybe we could stop by The Double Dipper for ice cream after we talk with Dan."

"Major cool idea, Leilani." Maile beamed. "I love the two scoops of pineapple sorbet drowning in fresh pineapple chunks."

Sam nodded. "Works for me."

My ears picked up the sound of Kainoa's old pickup.

Sam jumped to his feet. "Let's move it and get this whole questioning thing over. The Double Dipper is waiting." He jogged toward the approaching vehicle and waved his arms like he was flagging a winning racecar.

Kainoa pulled to the side of the road and our threesome piled in. After a quick arrival at the clinic, we unloaded out of the truck. Thankful we hadn't had to walk the whole way, I shot a smile to Kainoa. "Thanks for the ride."

"Sure. You guys want me to wait for you?"

Of course I wanted him to wait. The more time I could spend with Kainoa, the happier I was. The tug on my heart prodded me to say yes, but common sense yelled at me not to push my luck.

Maile answered and saved me the pain of making a decision.

"Naw. We're good. After we're done here, we're going to The Double Dipper."

"Hey, maybe I'll see you there. I was planning on hanging out with Tyler this afternoon."

"Cool." I prayed that I didn't sound ooey-gooey or that my grin looked goofy. I fled the parking lot and bounded into the clinic.

Maggie greeted me with a smile. "Everything okay with your arm, Leilani?"

"Oh, yes." I held it up. "All good. Just wanted to ask you some questions about yesterday when the Menehune was taken. Is that okay?"

"Certainly."

Maile and Sam appeared and stood on either side of me.

"How many people were working in the clinic during the time you went to the back?"

"Let's see. There was me, Dan the technician and ..." She pursed her lips. "Actually I guess it was only the two of us. Our nurse had taken a break and went down the street for a cup of coffee. Oh my! You don't think ..."

A shudder crept its way through my body and my heart dropped like a ripe coconut from the top of a palm tree.

Dan could have snatched both statues.

Iwakaluakumaha
(Twenty-Four)

I clenched my backpack straps. "Is Dan working today?"
Maggie nodded.

"If he's not busy, could I talk to him?"

"Sure. Why don't you have a seat and I'll get him."

Our threesome wandered into the waiting room and sank into a soft couch.

"Hey, Leilani." Maile nudged me. "I know what you're thinking. You're afraid Dan's the thief because he may have been at the library and at the clinic when both Menehunes were taken. But don't forget, there's that other guy you saw at the library and he also matched the description of the person your mom saw here."

"Ditto." Sam nodded. It was unusual for him to have only one word to add.

"You're right, but that other guy also matches Tyler's description. And he was working at Toy World when that one disappeared." I hung my head. "Don't want it to be either of them."

"How's the surfing, Leilani Akamai?"

I raised my eyes and caught sight of Dan's amazing smile. "Hey, Dan-The-Cast-Man. No surfing yet."

He settled into a chair across from us. "Maggie says you wanted to ask me some questions. Something about the missing statue?"

"Yeah. Do you have any idea who might have taken it?"

"No. It was a real shocker to all of us here. And now there's been others missing, so I guess the entire fundraiser is cancelled."

I swallowed hard and shot him the next question. "Were you at the library two days ago right before the fire?"

His eyebrows pulled together. "Yes, I was. I stopped on my way to work to pick up a book. But I was running late, so I left before I found anything to check out."

"So you weren't there when the fire started?"

"Nope. Heard about it on the news."

"Since you were on the team that planned the event, did you tell anyone else about the locations of the statues?"

Dan squared his jaw. "No. And the list is at the bank in my safe deposit box, so no one has had access to it."

I stood and smiled. "Sorry. Had to ask these things. We're talking to everyone on the committee."

His stern face melted into a soft smile. "Oh, yeah. Since you three kids figured out the secret of the pineapple fields, you think you can solve every mystery, huh?"

Narrowing my eyes, I sent him a lip-curl.

He winked. "Good luck, guys."

Dan-The-Cast-Man headed to the back and Maile, Sam and I made our way out of the clinic and down the street.

Sam started singing and rapping. He added a little rhythm section with his tongue, claps, and slaps to his thighs. His swagger as he walked down the street perfected the entire performance.

Glad for the relief from tension, I tried to join him, but had a hard time with the words and my notes sounded like elephant bellows. Maile just laughed. By the time we entered The Double Dipper, Maile and I were giggling like out-of-control hyenas. Sam smiled and shook his head.

I scooted across the small shop and lined up to order. "So, Maile's getting the sorbet with fresh pineapple. What are you getting, Sam?"

"Hmm." He scanned the menu board. "Thinking their famous chocolate double dipper with hot fudge in a waffle cone. Or … maybe a scoop of mango and a scoop of guava topped with granola." He shrugged. "Maybe I'll go big-time. Double chocolate ice cream, dark chocolate brownie chunks, and drenched in extra hot fudge. Yeah, cool."

Maile grimaced. "I don't think I've ever known anyone who loves chocolate like you do, Sam."

"Yeah." Grinning, I poked Sam in the stomach. "It's amazing you don't weigh over three hundred pounds."

"Funny!" He shrugged. "Don't eat it much. Mom hates having it around the house or she'll pig out. So, usually only get it on my birthday."

"Sam, you're up." I nudged him toward the counter.

"Huh?"

Sighing, I turned toward the tanned young girl with blonde hair, standing behind the counter. Her name tag read *Penny*. "Okay, Penny, he wants two scoops of the double chocolate with dark chocolate brownies and extra hot fudge in a waffle cone."

She shrugged and grabbed a scooper. "Not many people can handle one of those." She piled the cone high, then took Maile's order for the sorbet with fresh pineapple. I decided on the same.

We watched as Penny prepared each treat. As she handed

the wickedly chocolate masterpiece to Sam, she leaned forward and whispered. "Now, if you feel sick, promise me you won't throw up in the store."

Giggling, Maile and I clutched our sweet delights and headed toward a nearby table. Sam dragged behind. He thudded onto a chair and grimaced. "That Penny girl was a jerk."

"Huh-uh." A huge bite of pineapple and sorbet swirled around inside my mouth. I swallowed. "I think she was flirting with you."

"Really?" Sam turned his chocolate smeared lips and cheeks toward the counter.

Penny eyed him, smiled, and waved.

Sam beamed.

Maile tossed a napkin his direction. "Might want to wipe off some of that fudge."

"Oh, man! She saw me with all this crud on my face." Successful at ridding his mouth of the brown smears, he threw the napkin on the table and planted himself into the chair back.

"Come on, Sam. It's okay." Maile leaned toward him. "You looked cute."

He sneered. "Just how I dream of looking in front of girls."

Maile pointed at the humongous ice cream cone. "Show her how cool and manly you are by finishing the whole thing with no problem."

We tackled our treats, but before we got too far, I noticed two guys coming into the store. Kainoa and Tyler.

They spotted us, waved, and marched toward our table, Kainoa in the lead. "Hey, you three. Good eats, yeah?"

I nodded and tried to avoid Tyler's eyes. But he spoke first. "Hi, Leilani. Kainoa told me you were going to talk with the committee members for The Menehune Hunt today. Any luck?"

"Kind of. We may have eliminated two people as suspects, but there are still several people we're unsure about."

"I hope you can eliminate me as one of them."

A bonfire burst into flame in my cheeks. I forced myself to glue my eyes to Tyler's. "I'm sorry, Tyler, but right now I can't totally eliminate you."

He sneered at me.

I squeezed my spoon until my fingers tingled.

Kainoa grabbed Tyler's arm. "Let's get some ice cream, man. These three already solved one case and cleared several suspects. They'll figure it out and clear you too."

Allowing my lips to turn upward, I gazed at Kainoa. He defended me. How totally cool was that? I couldn't wait to get back to surfing and to have him help me with conquering the big waves.

"Yeah, I get it." Tyler turned his back to me. "See ya."

Kainoa glanced over his shoulder and passed me a comforting smile.

"Hey, Leilani, your sorbet's melting." Maile waved her hand in circles.

I shoveled in several spoonfuls and hoped the icy treat would put out the blaze still burning in my face. "How about we head home and while we're walking we can finish these gigantic things and plan what to do next."

Sam grimaced. "For real? You want to leave now?"

I noticed him take a quick peek at the front counter. "Don't worry, Sam. You put on that cool-dude walk and Penny will have her eyes glued to you all the way out the door."

He cocked his head and sent me a little lip-curl.

I stood, gathered up my stuff, and punched Sam's arm.

Our threesome wove our way between tables and out the door. Sam had a great I'm-so-cool walk going on. A couple sideways glances confirmed Penny was watching Sam the entire way. Once outside I nudged Maile. "I'm going to get us some napkins."

Inside, I spotted Kainoa at a table. I fought the urge to go talk to him, but I didn't want to be a total geek, like an adoring teeny-bopper. So I chose to send him a quick wave and head toward the dispenser at the counter.

Tyler was standing close to the napkins, his back to me, talking on his cell phone.

I grabbed a fistful of the tiny squares. As I turned to go, Tyler's words caught my attention.

"Yeah, yeah. Don't worry. I'll be there. See you tonight around eight at the harbor."

Iwakaluakumalima
(Twenty-Five)

Hand planted across my mouth, I scurried out of The Double Dipper. I worried whether the pineapple-drenched sorbet I'd eaten would stay put. Maile and Sam turned as I burst through the door and onto the sidewalk.

Maile gawked at me. "What's wrong? You look terrible."

Stomach raging, I opened my mouth and sputtered words. "I ... I overheard Tyler on the phone."

"Tyler? Who was he talking to?"

I shook my head. "Don't know. But he said something about meeting the person at the harbor around eight tonight."

"Harbor?" Confusion covered Sam's face for an instant. But then he waved his spoon in the air. "Oh, man! The diamonds, right?"

"Shh." I glanced behind to see if anyone was around. "Let's get going to my house. Do you think your moms will let you stay the night? Sam, I know Kimo will be excited to have you stay in his room. He thinks you're the best."

"Cool." Sam bit off a chunk of waffle cone.

Maile nodded. "My mom will say yes for sure. She likes you and your mom a lot."

"Perfect." I hurried my feet and tromped toward home.

Maile double-timed her steps to keep up. "What ya got in mind? Are we going to figure out our next move tonight?"

"Nope."

Sam scrunched his nose. "I don't get it. Why are we having this crazy slumber party thing if we're not working on a plan?"

"We're going to go on a stakeout at the harbor."

Maile's voice raised a pitch or two. "The harbor? Why? I mean, I know why, but isn't it kinda far away? Don't know how my mom would feel about me hanging around that scary place at night. How are we going to do this stakeout thing anyway?"

"Yeah, Leilani, how?" Sam huffed behind me. "And what's with all this super-fast walking? You practicing for a marathon? I can't eat my ice cream."

"Sorry." I slowed my steps. "Have either of you ever eaten at Palmer's Pizza?"

Maile moved from behind to my right side. "Nope. But I've heard it's major fun and the pizza is yummy."

"Went there once with the youth group. Awesome pizza and some way cool games."

Of course Sam would love it. They served food.

"Why didn't Leilani and I go?" Maile tilted her head and glanced my direction.

Sam shrugged. "Surfing competition I think."

"Yeah, I remember." Kainoa and I did really well at that one. A mental video played of Kainoa's amazing ride that put him in first place. I smiled and realized my stomach had calmed, so I shoved in a huge bite of sorbet and pineapple. The mini-movie continued to parade through my head, switching scenes from the beach to a family outing at Palmer's. It was one of the last great things we did together before Dad died.

"So, what's up?"

I smiled at Maile. "We're going to ask my mom to take us there tonight. Just the three of us. We can have pizza and play all the games." I paused and took in my friends' puzzled expressions. "Then we'll walk the short distance to the harbor at seven-thirty to see what Tyler's going to do there at eight."

The puzzled looks morphed into shock.

Maile groaned. "But that place is major creepy. Isn't there some other way we can do this thing? Maybe just confront Tyler about the phone call?"

"I don't know." Sam wiped a hand across his lips. "The harbor might not be all that bad. Besides, we're lookin' for a smuggler, not a murderer." He shrugged. "Doubt there'll be much danger." He belched long and loud.

I winced. "Disgusting, Sam."

He ignored me, shoved in another bite, and mumbled the words through ice cream and thick fudge. "I'm up for a stakeout. And Palmer's Pizza sounds way cool."

"Of course Sam's up for it. Anything with food." Maile scowled and stomped harder as we walked. "Guess I'm outvoted. But you, Miss-Super-Sleuth had better not go jumping out of the dark and attacking anyone."

"I *do not* intend on confronting anyone." Cocking my head, I tapped a finger on my spoon. "Unless the guy is small and I think I can take him."

"You dork!" Maile swatted me.

I giggled, then devoured the last of my yummy treat.

Opening the screen door, I yelled. "Hey, Mom! I'm home."

Her footsteps padded down the hall. "Hi, sweetie." She maneuvered toward the kitchen. "You kids hungry?"

I grabbed my stomach and groaned. "No, I'm good."

Maile and Sam echoed my groan and words. Was Sam actually full? First time I'd seen him turn down an invitation to eat.

"Mom, can Maile and Sam spend the night?" I followed her into the kitchen.

"Sure." She turned and winked at Sam. "Kimo's going to be thrilled. You haven't stayed over in a long time."

Sam nodded. "Kimo's cool and kinda funny."

Mom chuckled. "You been practicing your burping. 'Cause you know he's going to challenge you."

Sam laughed. "I'm up for it."

"Other than Sam and Kimo's burping contest, you three got any plans?"

Trying to look like it wasn't a big deal, I shrugged. "Kinda. If you can drive us, we were thinking Palmer's Pizza tonight."

"Oh, I see. Just you three, huh?" She made her way to the fridge and stared inside. "So I guess Kimo and I will have to settle for leftovers."

"Thanks." I turned and motioned to Maile and Sam. Once we made it to my room, we crashed onto the bed.

Maile opened her phone. Sam did the same. Both had positive responses about the sleepover.

"My mom's going to drop off my stuff later." Maile pocketed her phone and glanced at Sam. "She said she'd call your mom and get your things too."

"Cool."

I opened the nightstand drawer and pulled out my notebook and a pencil. "Let's figure out what we need to do after the stakeout tonight."

Maile's eyebrows pulled together. "Doesn't that depend on what we learn from Tyler and the mystery person at the harbor?"

"Yeah, I guess so. Sorry, guys. I'm totally ready to figure out this whole mess."

Maile squirmed and readjusted her position. "I'm just glad the police haven't shown up at our houses after what Mrs. Wong said the other day."

"I think the detectives figure she's a crazy lady and aren't taking her seriously."

"Hope you're right, 'cause my mom will go insane if the police show up. And then she'll ground me from everything forever." Maile frowned. "I may have had a better time surviving Mrs. Wong's dungeon than Mom's grounding."

Sam howled. "Ditto!"

All three of us let out pent-up anxiety by laughing and thrashing around.

"Ouch!" I smacked into Maile's head.

She rubbed her forehead. "Sorry, Leilani."

Mom knocked, and then poked her head into the room. "Here are the packs your mom dropped off, Maile." She deposited the two bags inside the door.

"Thanks Mrs. Akamai." Maile stood and snatched hers, tossing the other to Sam.

Mom glanced at her watch. "You about ready to head out?"

I stood. "Yeah. We'll be there in a minute."

"Kimo and I will meet you in the car." She shut the door.

My tummy still ached from too much sorbet, but we had to get going in order to be at the harbor in time for Tyler's meeting.

Sam opened his pack, dumped the clothes and toothpaste out, and slipped the straps over one shoulder. "Let's do this." He marched toward the door.

"With ya, Sam." Maile went through the same routine with

her bag and headed out.

I followed behind, a grin spreading my lips wide. The harbor stakeout tonight scared me, but the thought also excited me. Maybe we'd catch a diamond smuggler and Menehune statue thief tonight.

My friends and I piled out of the SUV.

Nerves spiked, causing my hands to shake and my mouth go dry. I swallowed hard and glanced at Mom.

"You kids have fun and call me when you're ready to come home. But no later than ten, okay?"

"No pro-blem-o, Mrs. Akamai." Sam bounded toward the restaurant and hollered over his shoulder. "Thanks for the ride."

Maile and I jogged after him, catching up as he opened the heavy wooden front door. Pizza aromas found my nose and the bells, thuds, and crashes of games thundered in my ears.

Eyes closed, Maile sucked in a huge breath. "Yum! Can't believe the pizza smells so good after all the sweet stuff we ate this afternoon."

"Ice cream's nothin' but a treat. Pizza's dinner." Sam surveyed the room and pointed. "There's a table. Want to order now or play games? Me — I'd go for games. The greatest ever is bowling into the different rings. 'Course, never can get the stupid thing into the center spot. You guys got a favorite?"

My mouth opened, but I had no chance to get anything out. Sam's words plowed right over me.

"Pinball's fun too. Really cool your mom gave us money."

"Okay, Sam. We get it. Why don't we play some games first and then order pizza." I pointed. "Looks like the one you like is open right now."

"Way cool!" Sam dashed toward the room and anchored a spot in front of his favorite.

Maile positioned herself next to Sam and plunked some coins into the slot. "You go first and then I'll see if I can beat your score."

"Funny! Just told you I'm terrible at this game."

"Yeah, but I never told you how my balls seem to totally avoid the rings and dump into the reject hole."

Sam sneered at Maile and grabbed a ball. His first toss landed in the center hole. "Cool!" He turned toward Maile who glared at him, hands planted solidly on each hip. "For real, I've never gotten it into that stupid center hole before."

I laughed. "Come on, you two. Finish the game."

Sam continued to toss. Most of them made it into the lower scoring rings, but his last toss landed the ball in the center again. He whooped, yelled, and glanced at a scowling Maile. "Don't care. I'm totally into this hitting-the-center-hole thing."

Maile's grimace shifted into a slight smile. She snatched her first ball and tossed it. It went down the hole to nowhere. She groaned. "Man! Thought maybe I'd have better luck too."

"Go for it!" Sam slapped her shoulder.

Maile continued to toss. Most made it into the lower scoring rings, but her last ball landed right in the center. "Yes!"

I joined my friends in their crazy celebration.

"One more time, guys." Sam locked eyes with me. "You playing?"

"Why don't I go order a pizza. That way it'll be ready when we're done. Pepperoni okay?"

"Great." Sam passed Maile a look laced with challenge. "You first."

Chuckling, I turned and trudged out of the game room. The

place had filled up. I glanced around to see if any tables were still open. A tall guy lumbering through the front door caught my eye.

Dan-The-Cast-Man.

My stomach performed a cartwheel. In spite of the anxiety, I decided to press forward and say hi. I wove my way through tables, chairs and people. Dan had maneuvered a similar obstacle course and was now in a corner talking with one of the waiters.

I moved closer until I could hear his voice.

"Glad things are going well here." Dan cleared his throat. "I got hold of the last statue and now I have a little business to take care of at the harbor tonight."

Iwakaluakumaono
(Twenty-Six)

I raced back to my friends and smacked into the battling duo from behind.

"Hey!" Maile's ball spun wild. "You ruined my shot, Leilani." The wooden sphere bounced and landed in the center ring. "Yaaaay!" She bounced around in a circle, squealing like a little kid at a birthday luau. "Can you do that again?"

"Doubt it. You'll have to figure it out on your own." I waved both hands at them. "You'll never guess who I just saw come in here."

"You know I'm no good at guessing games." Maile grabbed a ball. "Spill it."

"Dan-The-Cast-Man. When I saw him I tried to get across the room to say hi, but before I caught up, he stopped and talked with a waiter." I inhaled a big breath. "I heard him tell the guy he had the last Menehune and that now he had some business to take care of at the harbor tonight."

Sam gasped. "He's the one meeting Tyler?"

"Don't know for sure, since I never heard Tyler or Dan mention a name."

A frown crossed Maile's lips. "Who was the waiter? Did you recognize him?"

"Nope. But I didn't get a good look. I was too focused on Dan."

"So now we have another suspect. This whole thing is getting crazy."

I sighed. "Yeah. Why don't you two finish your game and I'll try again to get the pizza and a table. Then we can talk more about the case."

"Cool." Sam watched Maile's final ball bang around and fall into a high scoring ring. "I like lots of tomatoes on pizza. Make sure they're on the side. Hate it when they're cooked." He tossed a ball and it bounced into an outer ring. "Great. Maile's gonna beat me this time."

Chuckling, I turned and marched in pursuit of *Mission Pizza*. The guy at the counter took my order and filled a pitcher with root beer. I paid and made my way to the closest empty table.

Maile and Sam trudged toward me. From the beaming look on Maile's face and the scowl on Sam's, I figured Maile won the war. "Hey, you two want hot chilies or parmesan cheese?"

Sam plopped onto a chair. "Both."

"I'll get them." Maile deposited her backpack on a seat. "Napkins too." She giggled. "I always make a mess with pizza. The sauce squirts out and usually ends up on my top or shorts. Especially if they're white. Hate that." She glanced at me and frowned. "But then you probably don't ever drip anything." She turned and hustled toward the counter.

Sam smirked. "You girls are crazy. Tomato sauce on your shirt is proof of a great pizza."

I grinned. "You would think that. Just don't mention it to Kimo or he'll start spilling on purpose."

"He was pretty bummed about not coming with us tonight, huh?"

"Yeah, but my mom will do something special for just the two of them."

Maile returned with a fistful of packets and the other hand clutching a big stack of napkins.

Our pizza number sounded on the loudspeaker. I scooted my chair. "That's us."

Maile waved her hand and did an about-face. "I'll get it."

Sam eyed me. "Did you remember tomatoes on the side?"

"Yup. I wouldn't forget that 'cause I hate them cooked too."

Sam rambled on about pizzas. What he liked and didn't like and why.

My mind shifted into detective mode. Replaying in my head the events of the past few days, I made a new list of suspects and their alibis or lack of them. The sound of a metal pan hitting the tabletop jarred me from my thoughts.

"Great!" Sam grabbed a slice. Gooey cheese stretched in long strings before detaching from the pizza.

A pile of chili, parmesan and tomatoes decorated the top of my slice. While the hot piece cooled, I shifted my position, placed elbows on the table, and supported my chin with both hands.

"So what does our suspect list look like now?" Maile grabbed two tomato slices.

"Been thinking about it. At first I had Tyler at the top of the list, but now I think Dan is up there with him."

"What about Tyler's cousin, Jeremy?"

"He's next. The rest of the possible suspects have pretty good alibis, so they're lowest on the list. But now we have to add a mystery suspect, the waiter Dan talked to. And then there's the person Tyler talked to on the phone, but it looks like that person is Dan." A big bite of the cooled pizza made it to my mouth.

Maile chomped on her slice and red sauce squirted everywhere. Most of it landed on her white tank. She groaned. "Man! See what I mean?"

I laughed, but Sam grinned and nodded his head. "Proves my point. Great pizza."

"Not funny." She blotted it with a napkin. "I love this top. Just bought it too."

We made it through the rest of the pizza without another sauce accident. I checked my cell for the time. "We need to go."

Sam glanced around. "Dan still here?"

"I don't know, but bet we'll see him at the harbor." I stacked the cups and grabbed the pitcher. "We want to get there early so we can see who arrives. That way we can follow them and catch them doing whatever it is they're planning."

Once we were outside, I noticed the darkening sky. The sun had set and a murky gray blanketed the island. We trudged along.

"I think I'm scared already and we haven't even gotten to the harbor yet." Maile clamped her arms across her chest and shivered.

"You'll be okay." I tweaked her cheek.

"That's not what's bothering me. It's the harbor and knowing there is a real criminal who might be there tonight. When I watch TV, those smugglers are always creepy."

Sam shook his head. "Maile, you're a dork. That's fiction. We're staking out a real-life person. He'll look normal."

A groan simmered in my throat. "Yeah. Like Tyler … or Dan."

Smells of the harbor attacked my nose. Boat fuel, fish and salt water. But the fuel was the grossest. No pleasant scenery.

Only cement walls, docks and a few boats.

"Yuck!" Maile plugged her nose. "Couldn't they plant some flowers or something?"

I yanked my friend's arm. "Come on. Looks like there's a place near the parking lot where we can hide until we spot either Tyler or Dan."

Our threesome plodded toward the large blacktopped area. The more I breathed the yucky air, the less horrible it seemed. Scanning the scene, I noticed a few cars, but no people.

"Hey, Leilani, those bushes along the edge of the lot seem like a great place to hide." Maile waved her hand, then coughed. "I hate this awful stink."

"Hang in there. You'll get used to it."

"Yeah, right. I don't even want to *think* about getting used to this ugly place and its gross smells."

Sam nudged me. "Let's hide now. Gettin' a little nervous about all this."

I lead the group to a great observation spot. Hunkering down in the dirt, I peered between bushes to inspect the large expanse beyond.

"Hey!" Sam gasped, then pointed. "Car's coming."

I leaned my head. Headlights approached. "Don't know who it is. Could be anybody."

The car parked along the bushes, about five spots away. A door opened and someone stepped out.

Maile craned her neck and whispered. "I can't see anything. Do you guys?"

I tapped my friends' arms. Once I had their attention, I placed a finger to my lips.

They nodded.

The mystery person stepped away from the car, but he

was still too far away to focus on any details. I squirmed and swallowed the lump forming in my throat. "We need to move closer."

"What?" Panic rang in Maile's muted voice.

"Over there." I motioned for Maile and Sam to follow, and inched along the vegetation in a squatted position. The night blanketing us seemed sinister, but the light coming from a random post spilled a little comfort into the gloom and helped me bring the person into focus.

I maneuvered to a safe distance from the car and settled into the dirt. Maile and Sam slipped in close behind me. I peeked through the bushes. The guy turned. He seemed to be scanning the parking lot. He paced a short distance and shoved his hands into his shorts' pockets. As his steps brought him closer to me, I recognized him. Jeremy Chin.

He was wearing a Mariners' baseball cap and a shark's tooth necklace.

Iwakaluakumahiku
(Twenty-Seven)

Praying Jeremy wouldn't hear my huff of air, I planted a hand over my mouth. He wasn't one of our main suspects, but as a committee member, he knew the Menehune statue locations. And now the cap and shark's tooth moved him to the top of the list.

But why would Tyler be meeting his cousin at the harbor? Maybe they were in it together, but I hated to admit it.

Another car approached. I took cover under the leaves. Maile and Sam tucked in behind me. After it swung into a parking spot, the driver stepped out.

Tyler Chin.

He moved toward Jeremy. "Hey, cuz. About time you go work, yeah?"

Jeremy glanced at his watch. "Soon." He stepped close to Tyler. "That's what I wanted to talk to you about."

"What do you mean?"

"We're going to need more help and I wanted you to apply."

"Jeremy, you know —"

"Yeah, yeah. I've heard it a million times, but I think you're wasting time working at that silly toy store. The night jobs here pay really well. Helps me cover a lot of my expenses at the mechanic shop. You know how much it's meant for me to own my own business."

"Yeah." Tyler shook his head. "But I don't have a business to worry about, and I'm still in high school."

"I know your dream." Jeremy placed a hand on Tyler's shoulder. "Med school costs some big bucks, you know. This job could make a difference."

"Okay. I'll think about it. But school's going to be tough this year and I don't know if I want to work anywhere."

"Gotta go. Think about it, man."

Jeremy turned and lumbered away. Tyler stood stoic for a moment.

Was he waiting for someone? Maybe the business Dan had tonight was with Tyler. Disappointed that the conversation between the cousins gave me no clues to the mystery, I rubbed my head and focused on the dirt around me. A car door startled me. But it wasn't Dan arriving. Tyler had opened his. He climbed in and slammed it shut. Within seconds he maneuvered out of the parking lot.

"Man!" Maile grimaced. "That didn't really help us at all. And where's Dan? Do you think maybe he was here earlier and we missed him?"

"Don't know. But my legs are cramping." I squirmed. "Let's head back to Palmer's Pizza."

Sam jumped up. "Sounds good. Can't wait to breathe pizza smells instead of this yucko air."

We trudged along the lot. Sam's pack bounced against his side in rhythm with his steps. "Maybe Dan's coming later. Maybe he's meeting someone we don't know since Jeremy's inside working and Tyler's gone." He groaned. "'Course there's always Edith the librarian or Carla the secretary. And Suzie from the library."

"I don't think it's any of them." I frowned in frustration. The entire thing drove me crazy. About the time we reached the far end of the bushes, a car turned into the lot. I grabbed Maile's shirt and pulled her behind a cement wall.

Sam leapt in next to me. "Bet it's Dan."

"Let's watch."

The car parked away from us, but under a lamppost. The man climbed out.

Dan-The-Cast-Man.

Maile squeezed close and whispered in my ear. "I wonder who he's meeting."

We scrunched in tighter and watched him from our hiding spot. He didn't hang around his car waiting for someone. He headed straight to the building where Jeremy was working.

"Man!" Sam rubbed his hands together. "Things are getting interesting. Dan and Jeremy must be in on the smuggling together."

I sighed. "Kind of looks like it, but we really don't have any clues that tell us for sure he or Jeremy is involved."

"So where do we go from here?" Maile wrung her hands. "I really want to clear Tyler so I can tell Kainoa."

"I know how you feel." I passed her a crooked smile. "But we need to be totally sure."

After Mom picked us up she let us rent a couple movies. Kimo joined us and, as usual, he spent most of the time jumping around like a bouncing ball, imitating the actors and laughing at everything — even if it wasn't that funny.

Partway through the first one we took a snack break. Then Kimo started his questioning. "Have you figured out who's been taking the Menehunes?"

"Not yet."

"Who are the suspects?"

"We have a few, but mostly we're concentrating on Tyler Chin, Jeremy Chin who's Tyler's cousin, and Dan from the clinic."

He plopped onto the couch. "I think it's Mrs. Wong." A huge grin overtook his mouth.

Sam nodded. "Yup! I can see that. Like she's smuggling and selling the diamonds to pay for her dungeon."

I grabbed a sofa pillow and smacked him, then Kimo. "You two are not helpful at all."

"Sam and I are real funny." Kimo scooted into the corner next to Sam and leaned into the soft folds of the sofa. "Bet I can figure it out. Tell me all the clues."

Maile clicked her tongue against her teeth. "That's the problem. We don't have a lot of clues. The suspicious guy at the library wore a Mariners' baseball cap and a shark's tooth necklace. The guy your mom saw at the clinic wore a Mariners' jersey. Could be the same guy, but we don't know for sure. Dan was the only person at the clinic other than Maggie, the receptionist, so he could have taken the statue." She settled an arm on the couch back and rested her head on her hand. "Tyler wears a shark's tooth necklace and he was at two of the locations when the Menehunes disappeared, but …"

Difficult for Maile to think about Tyler as a suspect. My insides hurt for her and for Kainoa.

Sam completed Maile's unfinished thought. "It's a bummer Tyler could be guilty. But good detectives have to keep every suspect on the list. 'Course Tyler's cousin, Jeremy, might be the culprit. Had a Mariners' cap and a shark's tooth at the harbor.

Could be working toge —"

I flashed my hand in front of Sam's face. He'd said too much. Kimo had heard it all.

A look of horror shined in Sam's wide eyes.

Kimo sat upright. "What? How do you guys know that Jeremy guy was at the harbor? Did you do a stakeout thing?" He scowled at me. "Does Mom know?"

Glaring at Kimo, I placed a finger to my lips.

He whispered. "You guys went there tonight while you were out for pizza, right?"

I nodded. "But you can't tell Mom. She'll kill me."

"Okay." He sent a sly smile my direction.

Oh no! Another opportunity for Kimo to blackmail me. He already knew two secrets from earlier in the summer. At least he'd kept quiet. He'd do the same this time. I only worried about what he wanted in exchange for his silence.

Sam sank into the couch. "Man! Spilled too much."

"It's okay, Sam." I leveled my eyes with Kimo. "So what do you want this time?"

"I want to know all about the stakeout and then whatever you do tomorrow, I get to go with you guys."

Moaning, I slapped a hand on my forehead. Queasiness gurgled in my stomach. "Okay." I turned toward Kimo and leveled my eyes with his. "But you have to do everything we say."

"I will." He beamed and moved his arms around in big circles, keeping perfect rhythm with his bouncing on the couch.

My little pain-in-the-pants brother looked kinda cute when he got excited. I poked his cheek.

"Should I bring my drawing pad?"

"Yeah, that's probably a good idea. Never know when we'll need you to draw something or take notes on conversations."

"Yaaaaaay!" He jumped up and zoomed across the living room. "I'm gonna get my stuff right now."

"We're starting the movie in a couple minutes."

His faint voice floated from his room. "Okay."

Sam looked a little down, so I gave him a playful nudge. "It's all good, Sam. Really. Kimo helped a lot with the pineapple plantation mystery and he's already helped us with this one. Maybe he can do something else." I paused and cocked my head. "Why don't we plan out what we should do tomorrow."

Maile adjusted her position. "I'm thinking we need to concentrate on our three main suspects. We should talk with Tyler, Jeremy and Dan. Maybe even ask them about tonight."

"Sounds good. I think we should see Dan first." I stood. "I'm going to get my notebook and make a list of everything. Be right back." I jogged down the hall and into my room. My notebook rested on the nightstand. As I reached for it, the doorbell rang. Who would be coming by our house this late? I snatched the pad and pencil and marched to the living room.

Mom was talking with someone at the front door.

Maile and Sam glanced at me, the same concerned expressions radiating from their faces.

Mom turned and I caught a peek of the man at the door.

Detective Yamada.

Iwakaluakumawalu
(Twenty-Eight)

"Good evening, Leilani."

I closed my half-open mouth. "Detective Yamada, right?"

Mom motioned for him to come inside, then shut the door behind him. "The detective wants to talk with you kids for a moment."

Trying to read the expression on Mom's face, I nodded. She didn't look panicked or confused or angry. Just maybe a little concerned.

"Have a seat, everyone." She turned. "Can I get you something to drink?"

Detective Yamada shook his head. "This will only take a moment."

After settling in, he panned between Maile, Sam and me. "I called the Onakea home earlier this evening and Maile's mom told me that the three of you were here. I called here, but you kids were gone, so Leilani's mom has graciously allowed me to come by even though it's late."

I gulped. "Why do you want to talk to us?"

"Do you think we took the Menehune statues — 'cause we didn't." Maile clenched her hands into fists and dug them into the couch on either side of her body. "I didn't do anything wrong."

Sam nodded. "Ditto. You call my mom? Bet she freaked. 'Course she freaks at everything. Did she yell and cry? My mom's big with the gushing tears and now she thinks her son's a thief." He sank into the sofa and planted both arms across his chest. "Guess I'm grounded for life."

Detective Yamada smiled, which seemed way out of character, and waved a hand. "No, no, you're okay. We definitely don't think you stole any of the Menehunes." He leaned forward, resting both forearms on his knees. "My wife told me tonight about your visit to the school and the questions you asked her about the statues."

We stared at him. Even Sam stayed quiet.

"I know you three solved the plantation mystery earlier this summer and that was great, but I wanted to tell you to be careful with this theft thing happening. It could be serious and unsafe. Remember the fire? The arson investigators determined that it was definitely started on purpose. Someone who'd do this could be dangerous." He narrowed his eyes. "You three kids should not involve yourselves."

I fixed my eyes on the detective. "We haven't done much except try to play the game. That's how we found out the statues were disappearing."

Maile seemed to have relaxed. "Yeah, and now the whole fundraiser is over because of the thief, so all we've done is talk to the people in the planning group. That's why we went to see your wife. 'Course we didn't know she was your wife at first. She's very nice. And she's not a suspect at all."

Eyebrows raised, lines etched into the detective's forehead.

I jumped in and continued the explanation. "Actually, she never was a suspect. Well, not totally anyway."

Sighing, he stood. "It's fine what you've done so far, but I just wanted to give you a little warning."

Good thing Detective Yamada didn't know about our craziness at Wong's market or our stakeout at the harbor.

Mom stood, her face contorted and her jaw rigid. "I am so glad you came by and shared this information with these three. They should not be messing around in dangerous stuff." Her glare stabbed right through me.

The detective made his way to the door. "Sorry to have interrupted your evening."

Mom followed him outside and chatted with Detective Yamada on the lanai.

Kimo paraded into the room. He hadn't returned after going on a search for his art stuff. "I heard what that police guy said."

I pointed at him. "Yeah, well, that means it's super important to keep our investigations quiet."

He zipped fingers across his mouth and pinched his lips tight.

Mom marched into the house, halted in front of us, and jammed hands into her sides. "What have you three been up to? You know I support all this Hawaiian Island Detective Club stuff, but if you're actually involved in something dangerous —"

"Don't worry. We're fine." I tried to keep my eyes riveted on hers. Very hard.

She shook her head. "I'm a mom. It's my job to be concerned about my kids." She pointed to Maile and Sam. "And I'm sure your moms feel the same. Now, tell me your plans for tomorrow. No sleuthing around okay?"

"What if we —"

"Nope." She flashed a palm in my face. "No arguments. Someone started a fire. If they're capable of that, they could do even worse. So I want a report of everything you're doing tomorrow before I let you out of the house." She tromped into the kitchen like she was on an important mission.

"Oh, man!" I slammed backward into the couch. "Everything is ruined."

Maile sucked in a huge breath, then released it. "It's not like we're doing anything unsafe."

"Yup." Sam shook his head. "Man! We were in more danger at the library with the fire and all."

"My mom won't see it that way. All she can think about is what Detective Yamada said."

Maile tapped on my notebook. "Why don't we start making that list of stuff to do. And maybe a plan for your mom to see."

I grimaced. "Doubt she'll let us out of the house no matter what our plan sounds like. And even if she says we can go somewhere, she'll probably insist on coming along." I flipped the notebook open and stuck the end of the pencil in my mouth. After a couple seconds of gnawing on the thing, I slipped it from my teeth. "First thing is to visit Dan at the clinic."

Maile squirmed which made the couch jiggle. "After that I think we should go see Tyler."

Sam nodded. "Yup. Then Jeremy."

I scribbled the last point in the notebook. "Hope we can get all the information we need."

Maile passed me a small grin. "We will. But now we need to come up with some ideas for your mom so she'll let us go tomorrow."

Tapping the pencil against my cheek, I sighed. "Maybe if we promise not to do any sleuthing …"

"Doubt that will work." Maile shook her head. "Besides, you don't want to lie to your mom, do you?"

"You're right."

The three of us flopped backward into the couch like limp saimin noodles. Kimo sat on the floor, cross-legged. Elbow resting on one knee, he balanced his head in the palm of his hand.

If we rode our bikes into town, Mom would know we were investigating. If we walked, it could take all day. Then she would really go ballistic. I sighed. There had to be an answer.

"I know!" Kimo sat up, his little eyes sparkling and his face beaming.

Iwakaluakumaiwa
(Twenty-Nine)

I stared at Kimo. "What do you know?"

He scooted close to the couch and lowered his voice. "How we can still be detectives tomorrow."

Eyes narrowed, I caught my lower lip with my teeth.

"I'll call Kainoa and tell him I want to hang out. After he says okay, I'll ask if you guys can come. Then he can pick us up and take us to town."

"Kimo, I know you like Kainoa and all, but —"

"He really, really likes me, Leilani. He even told me I was his bud and we could hang out sometime."

Kainoa was such a sweet guy. He treated my little brother like he was related to him. I remembered him saying something to Kimo about hanging out, but was he serious? Hated to break Kimo's heart. I shrugged. "I don't know if Kainoa has the time. Besides, if it's a primo surfing day I'm sure he'll be hitting the beach."

He laughed. "You're funny! Every day in Hawaii's great for surfing. I know he'll do it." Kimo jumped to his feet and grabbed the phone. "What's your phone number, Maile?"

She sent me a sideways glance.

I shrugged.

"Here, Kimo. I'll dial." Maile snatched the receiver, punched in the number, and passed it to the bouncing kid.

"Hey, Kainoa! Wanna hang out tomorrow?"

I cringed.

Kainoa must have answered yes, because the next words from my crazy brother were drowning in excitement.

"Cool! Can our sisters and Sam come too?"

How totally lame did that sound? I plastered my head into the sofa back and prayed it would suck me in. Maybe if I closed my eyes tight, when I opened them we'd be watching a movie and Detective Yamada never would have visited.

"Yup. You're my bud too. See ya tomorrow at ten." Kimo dropped the phone onto its base with a thud. His grin seemed to consume his entire face. "Kainoa's super funny."

"Yeah?"

A giggle bubbled in Kimo's throat. "He said we'll have lots of fun hanging out and for sure we can babysit you guys." The giggle morphed into a belly laugh. "I'm gonna tell Mom." He charged into the kitchen.

Maile sneered. "I think I'm going to have to whack my brother when I see him."

I smiled. "You know, I think Kimo is a genius." I motioned for my friends to stay put, and placed a finger against my lips. Tiptoeing, I made my way to the kitchen door and plastered myself against the wall.

I heard Mom's voice first. "Wow, kiddo. That's pretty nice of Kainoa. But do you really think he wants the girls and Sam tagging along?"

How did this happen? My annoying little brother who always wanted to follow me around had suddenly become the main attraction and I was now the tag-along. I screamed inside my head.

"He says we're going to have lots of fun babysitting those guys."

Mom must have muffled a laugh because all I heard was a big snort. "Okay, I trust you and Kainoa to take good care of those three. Now, why don't you get into the living room and finish the movies so ..."

I leapt across the floor and jumped onto the couch seconds before Kimo walked in, Mom right behind. She wiped her hands on a towel. "Anybody up for milkshakes?"

Sam rose to attention like a trained soldier. "Sounds great, Mrs. A."

Maile echoed the response and I agreed too.

"Mango okay?" She dropped the towel to her side. "We also have chocolate if you prefer."

I surveyed my friends expressions. Definitely we-want-chocolate faces. "How about chocolate-banana, Mom?"

"You got it." She took one step into the kitchen, then stopped and turned. "I hear you three are going with Kainoa and Kimo tomorrow to get some ice cream and hang out at the beach." Her lips raised into a sly smile. "Don't stay up too late tonight. I'm sure you'd hate to miss out on that little excursion."

Frustration simmered inside. I wanted to blurt out in a loud voice, *we're real detectives involved in a real investigation*. But then I reminded myself. I was a good sleuth, silently making moves, unnoticed by the people around me. Totally undercover.

Thanks to Kimo, we had a great cover story. I couldn't help but smile.

As I shuffled down the hall, regrets floated through my head. Why did I have that second milkshake last night? And now today we would probably end up going to The Double Dipper. If

I kept eating ice cream at this pace, it wouldn't be long before I'd be as round as a beach ball, bouncing around on the sand and bobbing in the ocean. I'd never be able to go from paddling to riding my surfboard.

Maile plowed into me from behind. "Hey! You need to move it. We have lots of stuff to do today."

"Yeah, I know. Where's Sam?"

She shrugged. "Still in Kimo's room I guess."

Sniffing the air, I caught the scent of pancakes. Maile and I headed into the kitchen.

"Good morning, girls."

"Yum!" Maile settled into a chair, grabbed a fork and stabbed a defenseless piece of blueberry pancake.

I joined her and before I could pour the syrup, Sam trekked into the room.

"Mmm. Smells great." He pulled out a chair, sat, and loaded his plate with four pancakes. "Love these things, especially blueberry. I'm way cool with banana-nut ones too. But my mom only makes plain ole pancakes." He squirted a load of syrup over his stack. "Sometimes we have fruit as a topping. Ever used whipped cream instead of syrup? It's good that way too."

"Sam! You'd better stop talking and start eating." I pointed at the oven clock. "It's almost ten."

He cut a huge chunk and shoved it in his mouth.

I slid my chair back and stood. "I'll meet you two on the lanai in ten minutes." I charged toward my room, nearly smacking into Kimo.

"Hey! You almost crunched me, Leilani."

"Sorry. I've got to get ready."

Kimo's voice faded as I continued on my mission. "I'm so excited to hang out with Kainoa. Aren't you?"

The thought of spending time with Kainoa gave me chills. But being his babysitting charge made me ill.

I stepped into my steamy shower.

Then there was the whole huge group thing. I would be sharing Kainoa with my two friends and Kimo. My mind took a right turn and focused on today's investigation. I quaked with excitement when I pictured us solving the mystery of the missing Menehunes.

After dressing, I snatched the notebook and pencil and shoved them in my backpack.

Maile, Sam and Kimo were waiting on the lanai.

Kimo bounced up and down, waving his hands and hips as if he were a Tahitian dancer. "Yaaaaaaaay! I see Kainoa's truck."

I nudged the little jumping bean and leaned close to his ear. "Hey. Don't forget. Not a word about the investigation." He gave me a quick nod before bounding down the steps.

Kainoa beeped his horn and waved a hand out the window. "Hey, crew! Hop in."

As we squeezed into the cab, Kimo questioned Kainoa about the day's plan. "What we gonna do first? Can we go to The Double Dipper later? What about the park so we can watch the surfers?"

"Whoa, big guy! We'll get to everything. I promise." He glanced at Kimo's face in the rearview mirror. "Was there someplace you three needed to go this morning?"

I swallowed hard. "The clinic."

"No problem." Kainoa pulled away from the house and headed toward town. "How are you doing with the Menehune thing?"

I shrugged. "Okay. But it seems the more information we get, the more questions we have."

"Probably the way it is in any investigation." He turned on the blinker. "The police called last night. Did they come see you three at your house, Leilani?"

"Yup."

"What was that all about?"

"Detective Yamada came over. He's on the library fire case, and his wife is one of the committee members who set up The Menehune Hunt." I shifted in my seat and stared out the window. "We talked with her yesterday and she told her husband. He was just concerned that this whole thing with the statues might be dangerous."

"Dangerous?" Kainoa flashed a quick puzzled look my direction.

"The fire was started on purpose. If someone did that, they could do something even worse."

"Makes sense." He turned into the clinic parking lot.

"Thanks, Kainoa." I jumped from the truck. "Can you wait here for a few minutes?"

"No problem."

I turned and hiked toward the entrance, Sam and Maile behind.

Something caught my eye — Dan.

He stood outside the clinic talking with the waiter from Palmer's Pizza.

Kanakolu
(Thirty)

Sam whispered over my shoulder. "What's up? Why'd ya stop? That's Dan, right?"

I nodded. "Yeah." My heart thundered in my chest and my throat went dry. Dan-The-Cast-Man a criminal? I wanted to scream.

Maile squinted her eyes as if trying to bring the two men into focus. "Who's he talking to? Do you know the guy?"

"It's the waiter from Palmer's Pizza."

"Oh man!" Maile groaned.

Sam allowed a grunt to escape his lips. "Now what? Confront the jerks? Think they're in this thing together? Man I hope they're not dangerous."

I gulped air and motioned to my friends to follow. "Let's go." Dreading confrontation, I plowed forward, locking my eyes on Dan.

After we reached the two men, Dan glanced at me. He smiled. How could he act so nice if he were one of the smugglers? "Hi, Leilani. Back again, huh? Is there something I can do for you? Your arm okay?" He tilted his head and reached toward me.

"It's fine." My eyes flitted toward the waiter and back to Dan. "I wanted to ask you something."

He shrugged. "Sure."

"Why are you meeting with this waiter from Palmer's Pizza?"

"What? How do you know —"

My legs wobbled. I prayed they'd hold me upright. "I saw you last night talking with him. You said you'd gotten hold of the last Menehune and that you had business at the harbor."

Dan planted his arms across his chest and pinched his eyes into slits. "You were there, huh?" He shook his head and chuckled.

What was so funny? Stealing and smuggling were not funny things, and neither was starting a fire.

"Leilani, I want you to meet my friend, Carl. He's a criminal justice graduate and is applying to become a police officer. I asked him to help me with this Menehune mess."

I closed my gaping mouth. "We know there are diamonds in the statues. Someone was smuggling them."

Dan dropped his arms to his side. "And how did you come to that conclusion?"

"We found them in the fourth statue."

"At Wong's Market? How did you ever get past Mrs. Wong, let alone have enough time to find the diamonds?"

"Long story." I sighed. "The important thing is we know about it. And we saw you at the harbor. You went into a building. Who were you meeting?"

Dan stuck his hands in his pockets and leaned against the wall. "No wonder you three solved the pineapple vandalism case. You're good."

I couldn't help but smile. My legs stopped the violent shaking and I relaxed my tense shoulders.

Carl stepped toward me. "Look, lots of the harbor workers

come into Palmer's Pizza, so I told ole Dan here that I'd keep an ear out for any scuttlebutt about smuggling. He figured the missing statues had something to do with valuables inside them." He shrugged. "Made sense to me, too, but I never heard any rumors. But because Dan knew the location of all the Menehunes, he snatched up the last little dude and found the diamonds inside. He only went to the harbor to talk with a supervisor there."

"Yup." Dan nodded. "That's the whole story, except the big-wigs working the building last night were no help. Didn't know a thing, or even suspect a thing."

An explosion of breath blasted from Sam's mouth. "Man! This whole case is totally weird."

"And that harbor is creepy at night." Maile scrunched her nose. "Smells bad too."

I stuck my arm out to Dan. "Thanks, Dan-The-Cast-Man. Sorry I suspected you."

"Hey, that's what detectives do." He shook my hand. "You looked at the evidence you had and made a reasonable guess as to what happened. Good job, Leilani. And your friends too."

We waved goodbye to Dan and Carl, and headed to the truck.

"What was that all about?" Kainoa shoved open the passenger door.

"Had to ask Dan a couple questions. No biggie." I slid in next to Kainoa. My favorite spot. But a little slide show of me interrogating and maybe even accusing Jeremy Chin played in front of my eyes. At least it wasn't Tyler, but suspecting his cousin could be just as bad. But I had to talk with Jeremy. He had access to the statues and he worked at the harbor where the smuggling was probably happening. We needed to hit the mechanic shop.

Before I could open my mouth, Kainoa spoke. "Let's get some ice cream at The Double Dipper."

"Yaaaaaaay!" Kimo sprung up and down in his seat, shaking the whole truck. "I love that place. And I'm getting the super big one with lots of toppings."

Kainoa grinned. "Could you be a little more excited, big guy?"

"Let's go before all the ice cream melts. Ha, ha!"

"Hey, Maile, would you text Tyler and see if he wants to come? He's a fanatic about ice cream."

So much for my plan to confront Jeremy. I figured it could wait until later. But the idea of more ice cream made me a little queasy. Didn't think I could handle another bowl after yesterday's humungous one, along with the two ice-cream-packed shakes last night.

"Tyler says, 'cool'." Maile pocketed her cell.

Kainoa drove a few more blocks then turned down Tyler's street. Shaded by gigantic palms, the street reflected thin streaks of sunlight. The shadow patches overtook most of the area. It seemed every yard had banana and mango trees. We coasted to a stop in front of Tyler's house.

The obnoxious truck horn didn't make Tyler appear. Kainoa turned off the ignition. "Looks like we may have to wait. Let's hit the lanai."

Everyone climbed out of the old vehicle and sauntered toward the front of Tyler's house.

I tromped up the steps and settled into a wicker chair. Kainoa, Kimo and Sam goofed around, punching and ducking and making silly sounds. Maile leaned against the railing near me.

She poked my side. "Bet I know what you're thinking."

"Yeah? What?"

"You wanted to go to Jeremy's shop. He's the logical suspect now. Especially since he works at the harbor. And he wears a shark's tooth around his neck. Then there's the whole planning committee thing. He knew where every statue was hidden." She hung her head and gulped. "This is going to be so rough for Tyler and Kainoa."

"I'm thinking the same thing." I sighed. Pain pierced my heart as I thought about poor Tyler ... and Kainoa.

Snatching a breath of sweet flowers, I glanced around the beautiful lanai. I spotted a chair in one of the corners. A Mariners' cap sat atop something else. I stood and padded toward it. After picking up the cap I grabbed the material underneath and held it up.

A Mariners' jersey.

Kanakolukumakahi
(Thirty-One)

I barely heard the footsteps on the lanai over the pounding in my chest.

"Hey, guys!" Tyler's voice.

Still clutching the shirt, I turned and found myself staring into his eyes.

He grinned. "Pretty cool jersey, huh?" His expression morphed into a scowl. "What's wrong? You look sick or something."

"No. I-I'm okay."

"I know what you need." He grabbed the shirt from me. "A huge waffle cone with tons of hot fudge from The Double Dipper."

My stomach flip-flopped. Already agitated from my discovery, it raged like Kauai's Spouting Horn at the thought of ice cream.

Tyler tossed the jersey onto the chair and turned toward the group. "Come on inside." He motioned as he paraded into the house. Everyone followed, except me, as Tyler's voice faded. "I want to show you this cool new ..."

I swallowed hard to keep my breakfast where it belonged. I should have confronted Tyler before he whisked his way into the house, but my voice wouldn't work. Kainoa was going to be so hurt about his best friend being a thief, a smuggler and an arsonist. I snatched the jersey and took a step toward the front door.

A car pulling up distracted me. Same car we'd seen at the harbor. Jeremy got out and lumbered toward the lanai. "Hey, what are you doing at my cousin's house?" He stepped close to the stairs and locked eyes with me. "You okay?"

"Not really." I wrapped both arms across my chest, the jersey swinging as I moved.

Jeremy waved a hand at me. "Like that jersey?"

"No, I mean, yeah …"

"Tyler told me he'd leave it on the porch for me to pick up." He winked. "Never told me a little cutie would be attached."

Even Jeremy's dimples couldn't save him from such a disgusting comment. I grimaced, but I really wanted to smack the jerk. "You borrowing Tyler's shirt?"

He laughed. "No way! That puppy was major expensive and it's all mine." He smirked. "Tyler would have to put in mega hours at Toy World to afford one of those."

The shaking in my legs hit warp speed. I glanced around me and realized that I had to face Jeremy alone. I prayed the right words would come out of my mouth. "You're the one!"

"Huh?"

"You're involved in diamond smuggling at the harbor." I ventured a step down. "And you're responsible for all the missing Menehune statues … and the fire."

He took a step up, his face contorted with anger. "You don't know what you're talking about."

Digging in my pocket for my cell, I put on the best I'm-so-in-control look I could. My hand shook as I shoved the phone toward him. I mustered up enough force in my lungs and spouted a deep, loud voice. "I'm calling the police."

In a flash Jeremy bounded up the stairs and whacked the phone out of my hand. It landed on the ground beside my feet. I scowled and swallowed the sour taste trying to escape my stomach. "Jeremy Chin, you were the person wearing a Mariners' cap and shark's tooth necklace I saw at the library just before the fire started and the statue was stolen. Then you were seen at the clinic the next day wearing your Mariners' jersey. You had opportunity to take both Menehunes. You were part of the group that planned the fundraiser, so you had the information on all the locations."

He moved so close to me I could feel his breath on my face. Did he feel the vibrations racing through my body? If he touched me I'd probably collapse. His words were slow and firm. "You don't have a thing on me. There are plenty of people who wear the same things I wear. And plenty of people who knew where those statues were hidden." He moved his face to the side of my head, his lips touching my ear. "And what's this about diamond smuggling anyway?" He leaned away and nailed dark, sinister eyes on mine. How could this horrible man be related to Tyler?

Nausea flowed like hot lava through my body. If I threw up right now, it would land on Jeremy. That would make him back off for sure. "We found them."

He leaned against the railing and settled both hands in his pockets. "I see, so the cute little teenybopper is playing detective again. Well, you have no proof." His eyes blazed.

I wanted to look away, but riveted my eyes onto his. "Yes, I do. My friends and I found one of the plastic packets of diamonds in the fourth statue at Wong's Market. And we were at the harbor last night and saw you meet with Tyler. Were you trying to get him to work there so he could help you with the smuggling?"

He moved in close again, nearly nose to nose. "You are one

crazy girl and you'd better be careful what —" His head listed to one side. His teeth clenched and the words hissed through his lips. "and *who* you are messing with."

I stared at Jeremy, my heart beating like a crazed rock band drummer. "Someone else knows about the diamonds too. Remember Dan from the clinic who was part of the planning committee? He got hold —"

"Shut up!" He grabbed my upper arm. His fingers dug into my flesh. "I don't give a blast about your worthless investigation."

In spite of the violent shaking, I mustered up enough strength to shove my free hand against his chest. "Let go of me, you creep!"

"Hey! You're a feisty little one, aren't you?" Jeremy's grip grew tighter. "Listen. I'm going to take my jersey and leave. This whole thing would have been fine except I grabbed the wrong box." He groaned. "I got a container full of stupid Menehune statues, and the school got the ones with diamonds inside." A laugh bubbled up from some evil place deep in his soul. "You and your wimpy friends can sleuth around all you want, but you don't have any concrete evidence." He pressed his body against mine, his eyes narrowed and nostrils flared.

Maybe if I fainted he would just let me fall in a heap on the ground, and then leave.

"Tyler's the only one who can say for sure that I was at Toy World. Otherwise, no one can identify me at the library, or at the clinic, or at any of the other locations. I even slipped by that insane Mrs. Wong." He dropped my arm and snatched the jersey. A wry smile formed across his lips. "So good luck with your brainless investigation, you pathetic detective wannabe."

Jaw set, I watched as Jeremy turned and headed off the stairs. Fuming inside, I leaned down, grabbed my phone, and yelled at the retreating figure. "I do have proof and you're going to pay."

Jeremy turned and opened his mouth, but a squeaking sound from the lanai distracted him.

"Hey, cuz!" Tyler swung past the noisy screen door and marched onto the lanai. "You get your jersey, Mr. I'm-always-leaving-stuff-everywhere?"

The set jaw and hard facial features melted away as Jeremy focused on Tyler. "Yeah. Thanks, man."

I shrieked at him, not caring that he was Tyler's cousin. "That's not all you've left here, Jeremy."

He shook his head at me, then trudged toward his car.

I held up my phone.

Tyler stood next to me, squinting at my cell. "I don't think that's Jeremy's." The rest of the group filed in behind him on the lanai.

Kimo danced forward, laughing. "Leilani, you're so funny. That's yours."

I nodded. "With Jeremy's confession recorded on it."

"What?" Lines appeared across Tyler's forehead.

Jeremy waved me off and reached for the car door handle.

Kainoa maneuvered to my other side. "Wait right there, Jeremy. Let's hear what Leilani has to say."

"I wasn't really going to call the police, I just wanted to catch you on video." I clicked on my phone and replayed the clip. Kainoa and Tyler stared over my shoulders. The sound kept recording even after Jeremy swatted my cell to the ground. After that, I had some pretty good pictures of the sky and part of the lanai roof.

Tyler locked eyes with his cousin. His voice shook. "Why?"

Jeremy yanked the car door open and within seconds he gunned the engine. Dirt, sand and small rocks flew from beneath the grinding tires.

Kainoa grabbed Tyler's arm. "We've gotta stop him." As he bounded down the steps, he glanced over his shoulder and shot me a quick command. "Call the police for real, Leilani."

Kainoa and Tyler jumped into the truck and drove out of sight.

I talked to Detective Yamada, and he immediately directed officers to get on the pursuit. Then he demanded a full explanation before he took off as well.

Kimo bounded off the lanai and bounced up and down. "Yaaaaaay! That was way more fun than ice cream. Weren't you scared, Leilani? 'Cause that Jeremy guy sounded mean and scary."

Sam chuckled. "Ditto."

Maile frowned. "You think my brother and Tyler will be okay?"

I nodded. "Yeah. The police will catch up with all of them."

Kimo shoved an arm in the air and ran in circles. "We're great detectives."

I plopped onto a stair and released a squeal of relief. I also figured that it would be a long time before the queasiness went away.

Maile squeezed my shoulders and placed her cheek against mine. "Good job, Leilani."

Sam shook his head. "Girls." Then he high-fived me.

Maile and Sam joined my brother in his crazy dance.

"Come on!" Kimo whooped even louder and motioned for me to join the party. "You're the bestest and bravest detective ever, Leilani."

I laughed, but didn't think I could walk, let alone prance around. Maile grabbed my arm and pulled me into the celebration. Surprising even myself, I hooted louder than the three of them combined.

Kanakolukumalua
(Thirty-Two)

After the party, we settled in on the steps for a few minutes to recover. "I think we should just walk home instead of waiting for Kainoa."

Maile and Sam agreed. Said they'd come by later to get the things they'd left at my house. They trucked down the road one direction, Kimo and I the other.

Kimo continued his wild jig most of the way home. I laughed at his singing and hollering. He even made up silly songs about the mystery and sung them at the top of his lungs.

"Have I ever told you how insane you are, kiddo?"

"Yup." He zipped around me. "But I helped you with solving a real mystery, huh?"

I nodded. "Sure did." I grabbed the bouncing kid by his shoulders. "And I'm so happy you were around to help." Did I really say that about my little brother who spends most of his time thinking up ways to irritate me? I poked his side.

He howled and wailed another song.

By the time Kimo and I rounded the corner to our house, the news had spread. Mom greeted us on the lanai. She leaned against one of the posts, a glass of lemonade in her hand. "Well, so the detectives return."

Kimo raced onto the lanai. "It was super cool, Mom. We're real detectives and we're real good too."

"I see." She leveled her eyes at me. " I thought you were going to stay out of trouble."

"She didn't get into trouble." Kimo to the rescue.

I was glad to have his help, especially since my mouth hung open in silence.

"She figured out who stole the Menehunes with the diamonds inside. And I helped."

"Diamonds?"

Words finally exited my mouth. "Yeah. The whole thing had to do with smuggling."

Mom waved us off and mumbled as she went into the house. "Thieves, arson and now smuggling. Great. Just great."

Kimo stared at me with beach ball sized eyes.

"Don't worry. Mom's just frustrated." I sighed. "She'll be proud of us once she gets over the shock."

"I'm gonna tell her about Tyler's cousin and how cool it was when you found that baseball shirt and how you questioned him and did that phone video stuff. You were like Velma on Scooby-Doo."

Yeah, Velma was cool, and she was the brains of the group. "Okay, but don't tell her anything about Wong's Market, okay?"

"But that was the best part. I did real good that day." His glowing face slipped into a grimace.

A knife seemed to stab my insides. I couldn't take away Kimo's amazing moment of triumph. I groaned. "Okay, you can tell her."

"Yaaaaay! He darted inside, a whooping noise exploding from his mouth.

Mom would for sure never shop at Wong's Market again, let alone allow us to go inside the place. I'd talk to her later.

I tossed my backpack onto the lanai and headed to the side of the house. Rounding the corner, I spotted my red longboard. Revitalized, energy splashed over me. Time to take the thing out and catch a few waves. Once I'd zoomed into the house and to my room, I dug through a drawer for my swimsuit. I found my favorite, and changed in no time. I slipped shorts over my suit and headed outside. After I'd grabbed my board, I hollered. "Mahhhhhm!"

Her face appeared against the screen door.

"I'm heading to the beach, okay?"

"Wait." She disappeared for a moment then pushed through the door, Kimo and purse in hand. "I'll give you a ride. I'm sure you're exhausted after all the walking you've done, not to mention the super sleuthing." She shot me a narrow-eyed stare, but her mouth curved into a lopsided smile.

We loaded the board on top of the SUV and headed to the beach park. Best surfing around. The short ride gave me time to think about the events of the day.

Lord, please be with Kainoa and Tyler ... and with Jeremy. I couldn't imagine experiencing the shock that had bombarded Tyler. But at least he had his best friend around to help him deal. I prayed Kainoa would have the right words to help Tyler. Maybe Maile would call soon and fill me in on everything that happened with the chase, the police, and Jeremy's capture.

Once we arrived at the beach, Mom helped me unload the board. I glanced around for a surfing partner. All the usual crazed surfers were there. One of them would buddy up with me.

Mom stuck her head out the window. "Call me when you're ready to come home."

Kimo waved wild hands out the window and made silly faces.

I returned a few then shook my head, turned, and headed toward the sand.

Before hitting the water, I settled under a palm, my behind sinking into warm sand. I tipped my head back and allowed the breeze to run fingers through my hair. Tropical scents of flowers and salty water filled my lungs.

I grinned at the little movies playing in my mind. The fire, the clinic, the police, Palmers' Pizza, the harbor, my friends and The Double Dipper. My stomach still cringed at the thought of all that ice cream. But the funniest thing of all was the replay of Kimo and Mrs. Wong.

I studied the waves a few moments and then decided to go for it. As I stood, a familiar chugging sounded in my ears. Kainoa's truck. My heart seemed to stop beating for a moment, then pounded double-time. I turned.

"Hey, Leilani!" He jogged toward me. "I called your house and when no one answered, I guessed you might be here." His tanned face glowed when he smiled. "Wanna partner up?"

Nothing came out. I just gawked at him.

"Leilani?"

"Oh, sorry." Had to make up a quick excuse. "I was thinking about Jeremy, that's all."

"Yeah, well, it wasn't great, but at least the police caught up with Jeremy and arrested him." He sighed. "Tyler was really bummed. Last I saw him he was with his parents. They'll take good care of him." Kainoa's smile broadened. "You know me. I handle stress by surfing." He turned, ran to the pickup, and yelled over his shoulder. "Be right there."

Surfboard under his arm, Kainoa trucked toward me.

"Good job with solving the mystery, Leilani. Man, you totally confronted Jeremy. And from that video he sounded pretty creepy." He smiled. "Amazing brave."

I lowered my head and focused on my slippers.

"Now you've got two solved cases. Must feel great to be famous."

Famous? Maybe in my neighborhood, but I doubted the fame traveled much further than that. Then a bolt of energy shot through my body. I was a real detective. Too bad school was starting in a few days. I'd be super busy. No time to run around investigating, interrogating and solving mysteries.

"Oh, I almost forgot." Kainoa dug in his pocket. "I picked this up for you since we never got to do everything we planned today."

I grabbed the envelope out of his extended hand and peeked inside.

Coupons for The Double Dipper.

I burst into laughter, and then I gave him a big bear hug.

Book Three:
Ukuleles Undercover
Coming Soon!

Leilani isn't happy about taking ukulele lessons. She's a surfer, not a musician!

But somehow her bothersome brother, Kimo, convinces her to go undercover as a new student so Leilani can look into the threats against the music school. With Maile and Sam by her side, she attends class with Kimo and investigates the cryptic notes appearing on stands, in cases and lockers, and on a bathroom mirror.

Existence outside the music school complicates Leilani's life when she meets the cute new guy, Brandon Charles, at school. She promises to show him all the primo surfing spots in the area.

As if Leilani's life isn't stressful enough, her mom develops a friendship with the mean math teacher from school, Mr. Edwards, who thinks Leilani should participate in the Math Masters club. Things get even more confusing when the investigation leads to suspect number one — Mr. Edwards.

From Chapter One of
Ukuleles Undercover

Dropping the textbook-loaded backpack on my bedroom floor, I groaned. Eighth grade was a lot harder than seventh, and the teachers didn't even care how much stuff they threw at us. Didn't they know we had more than one class?

Sounds of pounding fists on my door yanked me away from my moment of self-pity.

Kimo burst in, squealing like a hungry piglet.

"Leilani, you have to help!"

I leapt to my feet. "What's wrong? Mom okay?"

Kimo nodded, his face red and eyes bulging.

"You?"

More nodding.

I gritted my teeth and sighed. My irritating little brother was acting all crazy over nothing. "Then get out of my room."

He ignored my command and shot toward me. "It's my ukulele class. You have to come help us."

"I don't play the uke."

Kimo narrowed his eyes and set his jaw tight. "I know that. But you're a detective and we need your help at the music school."

"Ooooooo!" I grinned and made wiggly motions with my fingers. "Someone lose their music book or something?"

He blasted out a huge breath as he bounced onto my bed.

The little twerp was pushing his luck. "You are so in trouble, dorko."

He shook his head. "It's not something stupid. It's real important."

I clamped my arms across my chest and leveled my eyes with his. "Okay. This better not be some lame idea of yours."

"There's a big mystery at the music school. Some kids have been getting bad notes left on their stands or inside their cases. And I bet it's gonna happen again today."

"Bad like threatening?"

"Yup. They say stuff like, 'This is a warning. Don't come back here.'"

"Did you tell your teacher?"

Kimo's eyes grew into pancake-sized circles. "She got one too. And she was super upset. Then one of the moms yelled at Mrs. Lee because her kid got a bad note."

"No one has any idea why someone's doing this?"

"Nope."

Cocking my head, I puckered my lips. "Don't think there's anything I can do except maybe come watch your class one day and snoop around."

"That won't help." Kimo locked his arms across his chest and frowned.

"Of course it would. I might catch the culprit in the act."

"Everyone would know what you're doing, Leilani. It won't work." His eyes brightened as a sly grin wormed its way across his face.

A shiver flowed through my neck and shoulders. Whatever Kimo had in mind, I knew I wouldn't like it.

"You have to take ukulele lessons."

APR 1 1 2013

CPSIA information can be obtained at www.ICGtesting.com
Printed in the USA
LVOW100031110313

323552LV00001B/3/P

9 781938 388248